Mrs. C. Jenkin

**Jupiter's Daughters**

*A Novel*

Mrs. C. Jenkin

**Jupiter's Daughters**
*A Novel*

ISBN/EAN: 9783337032227

Printed in Europe, USA, Canada, Australia, Japan

Cover: Foto ©Andreas Hilbeck / pixelio.de

More available books at **www.hansebooks.com**

# JUPITER'S DAUGHTERS

## *A NOVEL*

BY

### MRS. C. JENKIN

AUTHOR OF "WHO BREAKS—PAYS," "A PSYCHE OF TO-DAY," "SKIRMISHING," ETC., ETC.

NEW YORK

HENRY HOLT AND COMPANY

1874

MACLAUCHLAN, Stereotyper
56, 58, and 60 Park Street, New York.

# CONTENTS.

## PART I.

## PART II.

# JUPITER'S DAUGHTERS.

## CHAPTER I.

### ST. GLOI.

"Calme petite ville, où t-ai-je déjà vue ?
Dans quel rêve, ou dans quel pays ?"
A. THEURIET.

In the spring of 1866 M. Eugène Delanoy
died. His death was an event that had been
daily looked for during the last ten years;
yet when it occurred it took every one by surprise.

M. Delanoy had been an old man as long
as any of his neighbors could remember him;
nay, he was generally believed by them to
have passed his hundredth year. He had
lived in complete seclusion at this Château de
Sept Ormes ever since he first came thither;
seeing no one, returning no visits, and holding no communication with the town, except
through his two servants, as old and eccentric
as himself. As he had lived, so he died, without either friend, or priest, or doctor,

M. Delanoy's death disturbed St. Gloi,
though it had long ceased to take any interest
in his life. In that far-away district religion
still held her own; and a death unsoothed and
unblessed by the Church distressed many good
souls, and scandalized even the indifferent.
Old stories were revived of his having been a
member of the Convention—an abettor of Bar-
rère's cruelties; for rumor seldom troubles
herself with dates or probabilities. It was
whispered, then affirmed, that he had left in-
structions that he was to be buried without any
religious ceremony—*enterré civilement;* that
after having lived like an atheist, he was to be
buried like a dog. Luckily, the old gentleman's notary arrived from Paris, and the town
was edified by a funeral sanctified by all the
pomp of the Church.

The St. Gloisians, as was natural, felt an
ardent curiosity about M. Delanoy's property.
What had he left, and to whom had he left it?
Was there more than the Château, its depend-
encies, and an adjoining vineyard?

The Paris notary was not, seemingly, unwilling to speak of the affairs of his late client.
Why should he, when they were in a prosperous state?

He therefore made it known that the heir
was a distant cousin—a M. de Saye—at that
moment in Italy or Greece; in fact, travelling
for his pleasure. M. de Saye was young—a
year or two under thirty, unmarried, holding
no place under Government, of no profession,

had, in one word, been waiting to succeed to
his cousin. There are some people, who, with
a semblance of infinite frankness, conceal as
much as they please. They seem to make no
mystery, to be not the least reticent, and yet
leave you as little informed as they deem fit.
In the end, this pleasant Paris lawyer carried
away with him much more information than
he had given. He had made himself ac-
quainted pretty accurately with the affairs of
the leading families—knew the figure of the
dowries of their daughters, information to be
imparted to M. de Saye, and other clients on
the lookout for eligible wives or daughters-in-
law.

St. Gloi is neither rich nor aristocratic, but
it is a thriving and most respectable third-rate
town. At the head of society are the Rendus
—*rentiers*, that is, living on their dividends,
and quite retired from business ; the Joreys,
iron-masters; the Chambauds, large wine-
growers; the Belairs, bankers, and a great
wood-merchant.

St. Gloi, not being a chief town, had but a
secondary set of Government officials, who
counted for nothing with the Rendus and
Joreys. In addition, there were some young
men in the lower grades of the magistracy—a
career always betokening some private fortune
—and the necessary complement of advocates,
solicitors, and notaries.

The St. Gloisians adored their native place,
and it was by no means unusual to hear them

1*

give it the preference over Paris. Nevertheless, they were intensely patriotic, and excused
the morals of the capital by asserting that all
the vice flourishing there was of foreign
growth, for which they thanked Providence.
The ladies had a sincere veneration for the
Bishop of Orleans. They had read his first
and second letter on the education of women ;
they preferred and held to the advice in the
second. Long before Monseigneur had coun-
selled the bringing up of girls on the knees
of the Church, the mothers of St. Gloi had
acted on that system. As a rule, the young
girls of St. Gloi were educated at the convent
of the Dames Dominicaines, a convent within
the precincts of the town. Madame Rendu furnished the exception by sending her only child,
Pauline, to the Sacré Cœur, in Paris.

Old Madame Jorey, Pauline's godmother,
had remonstrated, and the two young Mesdames Jorey had shaken their heads, but only
when out of sight of Madame Rendu. "It is
best to abide by old ways," said the old lady.
"See what has been the consequence of new
ones. Scarcely possible to satisfy workpeople ;
servants think themselves equal to their masters
and mistresses ; money does not go so far, and
we are fairly devoured and deteriorated by the
influx of foreigners." Madame Rendu answered once for all by pointing to that passage
in Monseigneur's letter which counsels cultiva-
tion of talents as a help for women scarcely
less efficacious than religion. Pauline had a

decided talent for music and drawing, and her mother would not have them wrapped up or buried.

The Mesdames Jorey held to their opinion, and said among their intimates, " We shall see what will come of it."

However, when Pauline returned home, no one could discover that she was a whit the worse for her sojourn in the Paris convent. Nowhere could you see more frank eyes, a mouth more innocent. She was like a fine clear sky—full of promise; modest, not shy ; willing to please, not anxious to shine ; nothing apparent that would lead you to imagine there were any finer elements in her character than in those surrounding her ; nothing to militate against her doing as other girls did, and as she was expected to do—marry the man chosen by her parents, have her trip to Paris, visit the Palais-Royal Theatre (that ambition of month-old matrons), buy new furniture to last a lifetime, and return home, at the end of six weeks, to settle down into a careful house-wife.

# CHAPTER II.

## NEW MASTER AND OLD SERVANTS.

It was in the beginning of June that M. Delanoy's heir arrived at the Château de Sept Ormes. He came accompanied by a friend, not even a Paris valet to disturb the equanimity of his uncle's two old servants, Eloque and Gonde. They were not man and wife, but Eloque was nevertheless completely under petticoat government. It was said, though who first said it was never known, that Eloque had a keen sensibility to rosy cheeks and smart figures, which often brought him into trouble.

Gonde, looking forward to a prolongation of her reign, took care that the first dinner she served to her new master should be in her best style.

"What a chance to find such a cook in this banishment!" said M. Vilpont, Gaston's guest. "*Mon cher*, I shall probably prolong my visit;" adding in a lower tone, "Suppose you seek information about any other amenities attached to your inheritance?"

Gaston followed up the suggestion by opening a conversation with Eloque.

"We saw several charming ladies this afternoon as we drove through the town."

Eloque grinned, and answered, "Comme ça, monsieur."

"Do they entertain much here?" asked Vilpont.

"Comme ça, monsieur."

"Any châteaux near enough for visiting?" Eloque grinned and shook his head.

For Eloque, the neighboring Château of Ste. Marie did not exist, inhabited as it was by Madame Jorey, widow of a manufacturer.

At an interview with Gonde the next morning the two young men were indemnified for Eloque's taciturnity. Gonde knew everything about everybody, and was ready to tell all she knew. If you were to believe her, there were not five just men in St. Gloi. According to her, every one of the fine stone houses on the Boulevard concealed a crime. "Where there's money, there's always a covering for sin," quoth she.

"Thank God," said De Saye, "we saw some pretty little girls not old enough to be criminals!"

"Pretty! does monsieur call Pauline Rendu and the Joreys pretty? To be sure, Pauline will have millions for her dowry."

"Are young ladies called by their Christian names by everybody here?" inquired Vilpont, with a glance of the eye that angered while it quelled Gonde for the moment.

"Why not?" said the old woman, with an attempt at excuse—"her grandfather was just one of *us.* They say he '*lent by the week*' during the great troubles."

" And the others you named ? "

"Oh! monsieur means the Joreys. They make the blue cloth for blouses. The father has had one fit; and when he goes, the girls (I mean the *young ladies*) won't have millions. They burn the candle at both ends, monsieur and madame. Monsieur eats and drinks, and madame dresses. Last new year monsieur took the stick to madame because she bought a gown with the money he had given her for the pastry-cook. But," said Gonde, suddenly changing the subject, "Eloque and I beg monsieur to say when he expects his new servants."

De Saye was amazed. " Why, my good lady, I thought you were both fixtures here? "

Gonde laughed sarcastically. " Oh! not at all, monsieur. We are both tired of service; we have saved something, and my niece at Lyons offers me a room in her house. One must have some quiet years to make one's salvation (*faire son salut*). As soon as monsieur could suit himself, Gonde and Eloque would be glad to leave. St. Gloi was not their country; they had only stayed from affection for M. Delanoy."

" You disappoint me," said Gaston. "I shall break my heart to lose you—such an inimitable cook as you are! Besides, I meant to have left the Château in your care; for you understand, I am not going to live here all the year through. However, I respect your wishes. Your going will depend on yourself. Find me trustworthy persons to take your place; till then I hope you have too good a heart to leave a poor young man without any one to care for him. I shall get into all manner of scrapes without you to advise me."

Gaston said all this with such a grave face that Gonde was half inclined to believe that he had taken her in earnest, in which case she must modify her declaration.

" Monsieur judged her rightly. She was not one to do an unhandsome thing; but she and Eloque were old to be the servants of a young master, and if monsieur had thoughts of marrying—"

Gaston stopped her—"Fate still holds a veil over the date of that terrible event, my provident Gonde—an event still more alarming for me than for you. I will give you fair warning. It wouldn't do to make my bride jealous; so let it be understood that your marriage or mine alone parts us."

" I like that Gaston," said Gonde to Eloque; "but they'll give him no peace till he is married. If he has any faith in me, it won't be in St. Gloi he will choose a wife."

M. de Saye paid a hundred visits in the course of that week. It is the custom in France for new-comers to take the first steps towards acquaintance, and De Saye was sociable by nature.

" Remember," he said to Vilpont, who

laughed at his ardor, "as a neighbor and proprietor, it is my interest to be civil. Some future day I may wish to come forward as deputy."

He found Gonde really an invaluable ally. The little old woman gave him not only the names of all the notables, but supplied him with such notes of their private history as would pilot him safely through the rocks and shoals of first visits. Ninety-nine of these were of a uniform tint. All the salons, and all the ladies in them, were alike; conversation and mirrors, dress, and tables and chairs of one pattern; no books visible; reading was considered in St. Gloi as loss of time. If women read at all, it was unavowable feuilletons in secret conclave.

The hundredth visit, the one exception, was that for Madame Rendu. First of all, she was not dressed for the occasion; then what she said was at variance with the formal and complimentary tone of the other ninety-and-nine calls. She was as little encouraging as possible to M. de Saye; while as to Vilpont, all the notice she bestowed on him were two stiff bows —one on his entering, one on his departing. Every one else had striven, by insinuating questions, to know who Vilpont was—why he was at St. Gloi, and when he was going away. The explanation that he was on a friendly visit to M. de Saye would have satisfied any but the dwellers in a small provincial town. They did not understand friendship; they only understood relationship. "A snake in the grass" was a pretty general opinion.

Madame Rendu gave herself no trouble about Vilpont, either as to who he was or what might be his motives for staying. De Saye was another matter. She was aware that she should be forced to think of *him;* from that there was no hope of escape, unless, indeed, he was already an engaged man, which she devoutly hoped might be the case.

Even while he was sitting opposite to her, doing his best to be agreeable to this difficult woman, she was meditating how to ward off his visits. She had made up her mind to keep M. de Saye at arm's-length until she was certain that he could fulfil the conditions she should require in a son-in-law.

Vilpont sat smiling and amused, watching his friend's efforts to please, and criticising his courteous speeches, which all fell short, like spent balls. As they were leaving the room, Vilpont's eye was caught by a landscape in water-colors—a beech-tree overhanging a deep pool, and a sunny distance.

"A clever sketch," he said; and going nearer to it, he saw the name Pauline in a corner, and a date.

Madame Rendu took no notice of the observation.

The two men drew a long breath as they issued from the house.

"What a terrible mother-in-law!" exclaimed Vilpont; adding, "Gaston, I pity you."

"She is solidly respectable," returned the other; "and that sort of woman has not a bad effect in a family."

"Not when she has a daughter with a fortune of a million."

Gaston shrugged his shoulders.

"'Sooner or later one must make an end.' This idiom means one must marry."

"Bon voyage," laughed Vilpont.

Gonde questioned Eloque every day as to what the gentlemen talked of at dinner; but Eloque had nothing to tell.

"They never," he said, "spoke of any one in St. Gloi."

Nor was Gonde herself more lucky in her listenings at doors or her interviews with Gaston; but she had formed her own opinion of her new master's character.

"If he marries Pauline Rendu, he'll never know again what it is to have his own way."

Eloque silenced her by one of his preternatural grins.

# CHAPTER III.

## INTENSE GOOD SENSE.

EVERY one who knows the habits of provincial towns will feel sure that De Saye's visits would be fruitful of other visits. The friends had not left Madame Rendu ten minutes when Madame Chambaud was announced. Pauline, and her friends Stephanie and Julie Jorey, seeing her pass, said at once, "Now they are going to talk marriage."

Madame Rendu, who thought the same, left the initiative to Madame Chambaud, and stretching her small person at full length on a sofa, exclaimed, "How easily tired I am now! What it is to grow old!"

Madame Chambaud smiled, saying, "At forty-five a woman may still have some pretensions."

"As to that, I prefer to be the woman of to-morrow rather than the woman of yesterday; age depends on character. I was born old."

The visitor shrugged her shoulders flatteringly. Almost every one flattered Madame Rendu, for no reason but that she was rich, richer than the people who visited her. It was a real disinterested homage paid to wealth. "You, with your income," or "When one's name stands before seven figures, quite

another thing for poor me," were speeches constantly saluting Madame Rendu's ear. And
though she said, " Ah! mon Dieu!" as if the
announcement were an accusation, and though
she despised the flatterers, she was tickled by
the flattery.

Before speaking further, Madame Chambaud glanced at a door communicating with
an inner room.

" She is in the garden with her inseparables,
the Joreys."

" I hear that Pauline is teaching them German, and she knows Italian also. You have
educated her, dear lady, for another sphere
than our poor town can offer."

" I hope her education has prepared her to
be a good wife anywhere. The only way to
keep women out of mischief is to teach them to
occupy themselves agreeably. That has been
our aim in all we have done. Rendu and I
are of one mind on that subject, and as for
other people's opinions—"

" I have always heard you praised for your
way of educating Pauline," interrupted Madame Chambaud.

" As to that, I don't know; but no doubt I
am criticised just as severely as my neighbors,"
replied Madame Rendu, who, having a good
deal of the strong personality of the purse-
proud, walked over her acquaintances (with
her tongue) without remorse.

In France there are many ladies, even great
ladies, who take on themselves the office of a

matrimonial agent. It is common enough to hear it said, " Madame Such-a-one made that marriage."

It is a disinterested service, the love of art for art. Madame Chambaud was one of these match-makers. It was she, who, with infinite tact, had made the elderly Vicomte de Trois Etoiles marry Euphemie Devrient, after she had reached the fatal age of thirty.

It was Madame Chambaud who had married a shipowner, fabulously wealthy, to little Ernestine Loanet, whom Madame Nature had made ugly, but whom Madame Chambaud, milliners and coiffeurs, had transformed into a piquante brunette, the rage for a season before and after her marriage. Both Madame Chambaud's *protégées* did her honor. Madame la Vicomtesse was at the head of various pious and charitable societies, and enjoyed the counsels of the most famed of directors. The shipowner's wife had taken another course. She had doffed her pretensions to beauty and fashion, and was now a *femme politique* with a *salon*, which was a rendezvous for the leaders of the Opposition.

We all have some *talent* which enables us to do some one thing better than others. Madame Chambaud had decided that *her* talent lay in marrying people. Once engaged in her vocation, her life became full of interest. She was always, as it were, in the third volume of an exciting novel. Her new heroine was to be Pauline Rendu. She had, ever since

Pauline's coming home, turned over in her mind all the young men of the department. There were the sons of the two deputies; the only son and child of a great manufacturer; the substitute of the Procureur-Imperial, a young man belonging to old nobility; and lastly the newly appointed Juge d'Instruction. But one was too young; another too old; there was suspicion of consumption in the family of a third; the fourth had assumed a *de* that was subject to doubt; the fifth was in every point unsuitable.

M. Delanoy's heir was the *oiseau bleu* sent by a kind Providence to marry Pauline Rendu. Age, looks, fortune, position, all as if provided by special interposition. She only hoped that Pauline's mother might see all these advantages as clearly as others did. Feeling thus, and in no way abashed by her rich friend's abruptness, Madame Chambaud went on complacently—

"Curious that M. de Saye is not yet married—he looks thirty."

"Probably he waited for the old man's death to be able to marry; these *sons of family* have seldom much besides their name."

"Well, that is something, particularly nowadays."

"Not my way of thinking," replied Madame Rendu. "My daughter has not been brought up to endure privations, and her fortune will not be large enough during our lifetime to make up for want of money in her husband. However, as I do not intend that Pauline should marry before her majority, the age at which I myself married, I have time for consideration."

" What a sensible woman you are! Really, even knowing you so well as I do, you astonish me. Few mothers—indeed, I may say none, in St. Gloi are at this moment thinking like you ; for instance, Madame Malotean."

" I should be delighted to hear of Isabelle's marriage to M. de Saye. It is time she was married ; she is four-and-twenty."

Madame Chambaud paid several visits after leaving Madame Rendu, and did not deny herself the pleasure of expatiating on the subject of Mademoiselle Rendu's dowry.

The simple conclusion to be drawn from what Madame Chambaud reported was that the Rendus did not intend to open their purse very wide at the young lady's marriage.

" Quite right," said some ; " expectations are what make good sons-in-law."

" But M. and Mme. Rendu may live these thirty or even forty years," observed the Juge d' Instruction.

" Yes, it's long to wait," replied another young man.

The Chief of the Indirect Taxes was Madame Rendu's next visitor. He had been one of the listeners to Madame Chambaud's report. He was one of your cordial men. He began—

" Ha, ha! my dear lady; here is just what

you require, landed at your very door—young,
handsome, well-born, and destined for a prefecture."

"Then you have not seen Madame Chamband," replied Madame Rendu dryly. "I have
recommended her to make a match between
Isabelle Maloteau and M. de Saye."

"Seriously?"

"Very seriously. We look for a fortune at
least equal to that of Pauline."

"And that is—?"

"Imagine! Rendu has never told me how
much; but I fancy M. de Saye would fall
short of our mark."

The Chief of the Indirect Taxes went away,
saying to himself, "Clever woman—sharp, but
hard; a wonderful clear sight. Ah! poor
Rendu!"

The young ladies had been discussing the
same matters from their point of view.

There could be no disputing that M. de
Saye was handsome; it was a self-evident
fact. His friend Vilpont was, on the contrary, open to criticism. He was one of those
men whose appearance was suggestive of
many readings, according to the age and experience of the reader. He had fine dark
eyes, deeply set; a thin, narrow face, and a
long nose. The mouth, that betrayer of character, was hidden by a thick moustache. He
was tall, of a wiry figure, and stooped slightly.

Of him Mademoiselle Jorey said, " He looks
like a priest."

" M. de Saye reminds me of the heads in hairdressers' shops," retorted Pauline.

" Every one says he is just the right husband for you," observed Julie.

" I won't have him. I dislike him already. Besides, I heard mamma say he would suit Isabelle Maloteau."

" I see what will happen," continued Julie. " Pauline will refuse every one because of that ideal she saw in Paris."

" True; I must wait till I find out if he is married."

" But you may never see him again. And if you do, and find he is already married, what will you do?"

" Then, I suppose, I must do like the rest."

" Papa had an offer for *one* of us," said Stephanie. " It seems it did not matter which —not very flattering. It came through Madame—you know who. The name of the gentleman was not to be mentioned unless one of us agreed to accept him; for he did not relish its being known he had been refused. Rich and young, madame said. As his business was in Russia, of course we said no. We found out afterwards who it was, and I could not have endured him. Only suppose I had said Yes!"

" You might have come to like him," said Julie. " Claire refused M. Nogent—at least, the letter of refusal was written—and then she said she would see him once more, and it

2

ended in her marrying; and now she tells
every one she *adores* him."

" I dare say we shall all begin in the same
way," said Stephanie. " If Pauline will not
have M. de Saye, I should not wonder if he
were offered to one of us ! "

" I hope he will marry Isabelle Malotean,
and save us all trouble," said Pauline.

" I think he is good enough for the best of
us," retorted Stephanie.

" Then marry him yourself," laughed Pauline. " I promise you my blessing."

Madame Rendu's voice calling out, " Young
ladies ! " put a peaceable end to a dangerous
discussion.

# CHAPTER IV.

## WE SHALL SEE WHAT WILL COME OF IT.

THE stagnant waters of life were distasteful to Madame Chambaud, and no place had a more complete coating of stagnation than respectable St. Gloi. Destiny loves contradictions. The active find themselves in a position where there are no legitimate openings for their activity; while the dull, or the lovers of quiet, are plunged into a vortex which destroys their peace of mind.

What a godsend, then, for misplaced Madame Chambaud, was the arrival of a handsome, unmarried, tolerably well-off young man, within a stone's-throw of the *octroi* of the town!

Madame Rendu might like it or not, but Madame Chambaud was not going to give up her projects. Whether it failed or whether it succeeded, the hatching of it would be amusing. Match-making to her was what flirtation is to younger women.

Though one dinner painfully resembled another—the same dishes, the same guests, the same conversation, nourished entirely on local gossip—nevertheless, an invitation never failed to raise a ripple on the Dead Sea of the society of St. Gloi. The ripples became waves when

M. and Mme. Chambaud sent out cards for a dinner which no one doubted was given in honor of M. de Saye.

Madame Rendu at once proposed to send an apology.

"Why should we refuse?" asked M. Rendu.

And Pauline exclaimed—

"We have only been out twice since New Year's Day, and this is June!"

Madame made no direct reply. She said—

"You have nothing fresh to wear; and it is throwing money away to buy dresses to let them grow shabby in wardrobes."

"White muslin washes and wears forever," urged Pauline.

"There is no time to get a new dress made; and if I did order one, it would be the town-talk."

"We could get one from Paris, mamma. We have only to write to Madame Roger."

"No gossiping then with the Joreys."

Pauline did not need a second bidding. When she showed her note to her mother, Madame Rendu remarked—

"What French!—as clear as Chinese! The ladies of the Sacré Cœur have not taught you to express yourself in your own language."

"*Chère maman*, do you think we ever had to write about dress and ribbons? You praised my themes on religion and morals; now didn't you?"

Madame Rendu put Pauline on one side, and wrote herself to Madame Roger.

The Chambauds received no excuses; every one accepted. Two strangers—what a boon!

At the dinner, all the attentions were for De Saye. He sat on the right of his hostess, and on his other hand was Madame Rendu, a diplomatic move of Madame Chambaud.

As for Vilpont, merely invited as De Saye's satellite, his place was at the end of the table, among the juniors, and with those on the lowest rung of the ladder of official hierarchy. He was seated between a fat, rosy young matron and Pauline Rendu. His duty, and he knew it, was in no way towards the latter; besides, he looked on her as belonging to De Saye.

Pauline, in her new dress from Paris, was an attractive little person. Of all unfathomable phenomena, none greater than that secret personal influence we name attraction. It is not due to beauty, for ofttimes it exists independently of beauty. Emerson says, "In chosen men and women, I find somewhat in form and speech and manners which is not of their person or family, but of a human catholic and spiritual character, and we love them as we do the sky." Pauline belonged to this class; and it was, indeed, a common saying in St. Gloi, "that it was difficult to believe she was the child of the Rendus."

Something of the school-girl still lingered in her sayings and doings, and she was yet in the period of sudden dashes out of the depths of shyness to the front rank of audacious candor.

The fat young madame was singularly uninteresting; still, all the laws of etiquette bound Vilpont to address his conversation to her. She answered all he said by a short laugh. Driven to extremity, he at last spoke with admiration of the wreath on her head.

"It was got for the Woods-and-Forests' ball," she said, "and it never took place, because his father died. It was very annoying."

"Most people do think it an annoyance to die," he said gravely.

"I don't mean that, but that I had bought the wreath for nothing; I was so thankful when I got the Chamband's invitation."

"Ah! I understand now," said Vilpont, his attention engrossed by Mademoiselle Rendu's pretty hands as she opened some bonbon papers to read the mottoes.

Not once during the two mortal hours they had sat side by side had he and Pauline interchanged a word. The young madame, detecting the direction of his eyes, whispered—

"So clever! you have not an idea of all she knows—sings and draws, and speaks German. She was at the Sacré Cœur in Paris; an immense advantage, you know."

"I am glad to hear it," replied Vilpont.

He thought he saw a dimple suddenly appear and disappear in Mademoiselle Rendu's cheek.

Madame Chamband had a soirée in the evening. As soon as the dinner-guests entered the *salon*, the two Joreys rushed at Pauline, eager to know all that had passed at dinner. By whom had Pauline sat?

"M. Vilpont was on my right, and one of M. Chambaud's clerks on my left. The first did not think me worth speaking to, and the last was afraid to do so. It was amusing enough. Madame Gréemard surpassed herself; she told M. Vilpont the story of the man whose polypus was cured by sticking a piece of paper on the point of his tongue. I wish you could have seen the face of interest with which M. Vilpont listened."

"I do hate deceit," said Stephanie.

"He is not half so nice as M. de Saye," observed Julie.

"There's no comparison possible between them," replied Pauline with decision.

"I should not call M. Vilpont downright ugly," added Julie, "but he is so thin and woodish."

"And M. de Saye so wax-dollish, don't you think?" asked Pauline. "Oh dear! how I should enjoy it all if there were to be no playing nor singing!"

Vain wish! Madame Chambaud knew the desire of the hearts of mothers. What could girls learn music for, but to play in company? So the Joreys thundered through one of Vilbac's duets, to the admiration of their parents, who liked plenty of sound. Then came Pauline's turn. She had considerable musical talent, and a sweet, powerful voice. But, poor little girl! she displayed neither to advantage. She was seized by an uncontrollable emotion which paralyzed her powers.

Madame Rendu preserved a plausible show of composure; but the burning flush on her usually colorless cheeks, testified to her internal disturbance. Some good-natured soul among the guests, who, like many doers of good deeds, received no meed of gratitude, proposed that the young people should dance. M. de Saye, by Madame Chamband's will, danced the first quadrille with Pauline, who then took Stephanie's place at the piano, to play waltzes and polkas.

"It is a pity to see you condemned to play," said Vilpont, suddenly addressing her. "Can none of those ladies take your place?" and he glanced at a group of the middle-aged.

"I never waltz," said Pauline; "it makes me so giddy."

"If you persevered, you would conquer that feeling."

"I have tried often enough, and I don't much care to conquer in such a cause."

"If you have any polka or waltz duets, I am equal to playing a bass, and it would fatigue you less."

"Can you? that would be amusing. Just turn over some leaves of this book, and you will come to duets. Let us try to go on without a stop. How surprised they will all be!"

Obeying her directions, their four hands were soon on the instrument together—his so long, thin, and brown—hers so rosy and dimpled.

"You play well, and have a charming voice," he said.

"Yes, I sang so well just now! I have never dared to look at mamma since."

She might have added that she would still less dare to do so now. Perhaps half her present pleasure arose from knowing it to be against rules.

"My entertaining neighbor at dinner," he went on, "warned me you were a well of science and a mass of talents. I had already seen one specimen of the last, a water-color sketch in your salon."

"You are very easy of belief for a—Parisian."

"What was the word you replaced by Parisian?"

"Not a polite one."

"I guess you meant credulous for my age."

A faint blush answered him.

"You consider me then old—quite an old man, who may be allowed the privilege of playing bass to your treble. I suppose you wouldn't have allowed De Saye to do so?"

"Indeed, I do not consider you at all an old man?"

"Well, I am older than Gaston—drawing near the *mezzo cammin della vita*."

"And having met all sorts of wild beasts, I had a right to wonder at your being easily deceived," she rejoined.

2*

"I was not aware that young ladies were allowed to read Dante."

"I have read Dante pretty much, as I painted that sketch you admire. It's very provoking to be taken in about yourself, to find out that after years of school you know little, or rather nothing."

"I perceive you are a young philosopher, given to serious reflection."

"Do you suppose girls are blind and deaf, and never think till they are married?"

"Worse and worse. You are heterodox. Nice young ladies wait to receive their impressions from their husbands."

"That's nonsense; they cannot help seeing and feeling. I assure you, I have very decided opinions about most things."

She spoke with animation, and Vilpont thought her prettier with every passing minute; and being a man, that fact would have earned her pardon for anything she might be pleased to say. He said, with assumed gravity—

"I hope you are not imbued with, or rather poisoned by, the theory of the rights of women."

"I don't know anything of that theory; but I have ideas of my own on all I hear talked about."

"Politics, for instance."

"A little. I listen often to papa and his friends."

" And may I ask, are you Liberal, Dynastic, Irreconcilable ? "

" Something of all three."

" Now you puzzle me. Pray explain."

Here, in her ardor to do so, Pauline lost her time so completely, that she brought a crowd of complainants about the piano. Madame Rendu also approached the criminal, and Pauline, obeying the order telegraphed by the stern, black eyes, placed herself by the maternal side. She danced all the rest of the quadrilles with her townsmen, and behaved during the remainder of the evening with the customary discretion of French provincial young ladies ; but oh, how tiresome and insipid her partners appeared !

It was a surprise to Pauline that her mother did not take her to task about M. Vilpont. She had expected a lecture after the angry look she had received ; but all that Madame Rendu said was—

" How stupid of you to break down in your playing ! "

This indulgence did not arise from the shrewdness which depreciates by contemptuous indifference, but was the result of a preoccupied mind.

Madame Rendu had been told that evening that M. de Saye was disposed to live at Sept Ormes ; and it was also said the inheritance was larger than at first believed. If this were really the case, it might be worth her while to reconsider her former decision. She had

ganged him sufficiently already to be aware
he was not an eagle; therefore, the better calculated to make a safe, quiet husband for Pauline, and manageable son-in-law for herself.
It was this current of thought which restrained
her from attacking Vilpont, whom she felt
sure it would be better to have as a friend
than an enemy.

# CHAPTER V.

## FORESHADOWINGS.

IT was on the day after this dinner that Pauline wrote the following letter to Madame Agnes, one of the ladies of the Convent of Sacré Cœur:

"DEAR MADAME,—Do not be angry if I have not answered your letter sooner. I am very sorry I could not; but you must not be vexed with your child, she loves you so much.

"Whatever happens, my heart always remains with you. It is sad to feel my heart so full without having that other heart near me, to whom I could show all that is in my own. Do not answer me about this, for I cannot and will not let my mother see my feelings on this point. Dear Madame, always love me as you do now. It is such a comfort to have faith, as I have, in your affection for me. I consider myself very happy to have you for my friend.

"When I began to write, I fancied I had so much to say. You do not care to hear about parties; still I must tell you of one dinner at the Chambauds', at which we met M. de Saye, the heir, you know, of old M. Delanoy.

"M. de Saye is very pleasant. Every one speaks in raptures of him. He manages to be good friends with every one; even with the

Mayor and Arch-priest Gonnier. I am sure
they were never of one mind before about any
one or anything. He has no other particular
talent—I mean, he does not care for music
or painting. I know that Madame C——
wants to make a marriage for him. You guess
with whom; but that young girl will *never*
accept him for a husband—no, never!

"Do you remember I once told you I was
afraid of marriage, and how you answered it
was better for a woman to be married? But,
dear madame, take my place for a moment.
We poor French girls only see the man with
whom we are always to live two or three times
before saying 'Yes.' Have we not a right to
be afraid of the future? in particular when a
girl's life is so free of care as mine. Is it not
natural to be afraid to leave all that is known
for what is unknown?—what is certain for
what is uncertain? Must I not expect my
share of griefs in the future—probably in my
married life; and I must be ready to bear all
for a man who perhaps will not understand
me, and yet whom perhaps I shall love; for
you know I *can* love.

"However, I do not always feel afraid. I
wish to marry; not now, but in a year or two.
If I were not to do so, I should be desolate by
and by, as I have no brothers or sisters. Besides, I want to devote myself to some one.
Do not answer me about this. You must
think me foolish—perhaps I am; but I learned
in loving you the happiness affection gives.

Ah! if you were here, your counsels would do
me good. I embrace you tenderly.—Your
loving child,                           Pauline."

Madame Agnes concluded that her little
friend's letter was to be read as dreams are—
by contraries; and that this M. de Saye was,
after all, to be the object of that devotion
Pauline longed to give. The young lady had
somehow forgotten to mention the polka duets.

Ten days later another letter was sent to
Madame Agnes.

" Dear Madame and Best Friend,—On
awaking this morning, my first thought was of
you, and more than ever I wished you were
near me. I must now relate all that has happened since my last letter; first the pleasure,
and then the pain.

" Mamma decided that she would not give
M. de Saye a dinner, like every one else; so
we had a soirée. After we had danced, M.
de Saye's friend, M. Vilpont (who is now on a
visit to Sept Ormes) proposed we should have
some charades. At first no one would agree
to act, and then every one was eager to do so.
The first word was ' Cartel.' M. Vilpont said
the spelling did not matter, only the sound of
the word. So we had a scene on the deck of
a vessel, with the officer and men of the watch
taking soundings, and a lady passenger always
interrupting and wanting to know what they
were doing. I was the lady, and it was not

very good. But the second syllable was excellent. It was a parody of the historical scene of William Tell. Oh! it was the best of all. M. de Saye was Gessler; Stephanie Jorey and I were his guards; Leon Berthier was Tell; and M. Laroche his wife Edwige. He looked really like a woman. M. Vilpont was Jemmy the boy. Madame Chambaud dressed him as a baby, with a little cap. He came in on his knees, to look like a child, with his finger in his mouth. It was capital. No one would have expected M. Vilpont to be so amiable as to play this part. His face was so droll in the baby's cap, with his beard hid by a bib. Then we played " pompier—pont-pied." The second scene was from Cinderella. M. Vilpont was the prince, and did not seem at all flattered to fall at the feet of Madame Gréemard, she is so very fat. It was the best party we ever had."

Perhaps Madame Agnes might have been struck by the frequent mention of M. Vilpont's name, but for the end of the letter.

" Now for the pain.

" I am again discouraged, dear madame, as I am so often. I despise myself. I am tired of my own disagreeable character, and saddened by seeing I cannot make it better. I cannot help being impatient with those I live with. I cannot help vexing mamma with my impetuous ways, and it makes me miserable to hear her say I shall never make any one happy. This is what happened.

" The day after our charades mamma and I went to see my cousin Eugénie. You know mamma loves her as another daughter. We found her—where do you think?—in her husband's private room, where he sees his clients and writes. We heard very loud speaking as we were going in. Victor and Eugénie were sitting on a sofa, and as we entered we saw her give him a great slap. I shivered all over, but Victor was not angry a bit; he laughed, and said, 'Shall we have a separation, my angel?' and then Eugénie began to sob.

" Mamma asked what was the matter, and Victor said that Eugénie had been turning over all his papers, and reading private letters on business. Eugénie sobbed out that he received visits from ladies, and that she was perfectly wretched.

" Victor said to mamma, 'Believe me, I adore Eugénie, but she torments me to death; we must either separate, or I must give up my profession and starve.' I don't know what made me interfere; but I did, and I said that Eugénie must be silly, or worse; for if she believed her husband was a bad man, she ought not to stay with him.

" Mamma turned quite fiercely on me, and declared I was insupportable; that instead of trying to make peace, I added fuel to fire. I ought to have held my tongue; but I went on and declared it was wrong to make peace with badness. Mamma turned me out of the room, saying she pitied the man who should marry me. I have been so unhappy, ever since, to think that my own mother, who knows me best, should say I was *insupportable*. It is very hard to bear; and if you knew how hard I try not to be forever indignant—to be more quiet, like other girls! But I cannot laugh at things as the Joreys do. Pray write and comfort me. You never thought me insupportable, did you?—Your poor PAULINE."

No one can doubt what was the answer sent to this effusion. It could be no other than an exhortation to be humble, patient, and submissive; but the homily was so sweetened by terms of endearment, that Pauline wept tears of mingled joy and repentance as she read. Nor can any one doubt that she laid the counsels to heart, seeing how uncomplainingly she accepted her mother's refusal of the many invitations that followed the charade soirée. Her regret at these refusals she looked on in the light of a fitting penance—her own patient acquiescence was a salve to her conscience.

Madame Rendu was holding aloof until she could be sure of M. de Saye's plans. She prided herself on her far-sightedness. She explained, or rather told, M. Rendu, who permitted himself to wonder why they should thus seclude themselves, that she was the best judge of what ought or ought not to be done in the case, and that she acted thus solely in Pauline's interest. As for Pauline herself, Madame

Rendu unconsciously looked upon her as a puppet—eyes, ears, feeling, and understanding would be bestowed on her when she married.

In the meantime Pauline's imagination worked the more diligently for the absence of *reality*.

# CHAPTER VI.

### A FIRST SUNDAY AT STE. MARIE, AND SUSPICION LULLED.

THREE weeks after the polka duets, Vilpont, quite by accident, met Pauline at Château Ste. Marie, the residence of her godmother. Every Sunday all the members of her family gathered round old Madame Jorey. The French have strong family love. They say of themselves, "True, we laugh at matrimony, our race has always done so from the beginning of time; but in no country are parents more honored, the bond of relationship held so close."

Filial respect was especially great among the Joreys. The elderly sons were as submissive in manner to their mother as when mere schoolboys. Pauline was admitted as one of the family group by right of god-daughtership. Godmother and godchild are looked upon in France as connected by a binding relationship.

It was M. Edmond Jorey who had brought Vilpont to Ste. Marie, and who ushered him without ceremony into the *salle à manger*.

A pretty scene met the Parisian's sight. *Bonne maman* (grandmamma), seated in a roomy arm-chair, was superintending the handiwork of her two grand-daughters and of Mademoiselle Rendu.

All three girls were in *deshabille*, in gray

*peignoirs*, their sleeves rolled up to the elbow, and each with a spoon was rapidly stirring some concoction in a basin. The usual compact neatness of their hair was disturbed: wild little curls were floating over Pauline's forehead, and frolicking on her neck. The gentlemen had been watching them through the window for five minutes, and listening to their chatter.

" I am teaching them something better than music and dancing," said the old lady, her round face all in a glow with her own exertions. " Ma filleule (my god-daughter) has been looking after the gigot, which you shall give your opinion about at supper ; and now we are making three different kinds of bonbons, chocolate, pistachio, and almond."

" Will you let me be one of your pupils? " said Vilpont, seating himself on a footstool at *bonne maman's* feet, which also brought him close to Pauline.

He turned up his coat-sleeves, and with a sheet of paper lying conveniently near made himself a cook's cap. *Bonne maman* chuckled ; and the girls, how they laughed with girlish glee ! Pauline put her basin into his hands, bidding him go on stirring. At last the bonbons were ready for the oven, and *bonne maman* called out, " Run, girls, and get yourselves ready for vespers ! I hear the bell."

In a few minutes they were back again in their silk frocks and tiny straw hats, all wreathed with corn-flowers.

Vilpont—Heaven knows how long since he had done so—went to church with the family. He manœuvred so as to secure himself a seat on the bench immediately opposite to where Pauline sat. How innocent and good she looked, and how charming was her little *gaucherie* as she knelt on the straw chair, conscious of the short dress which betrayed her pretty feet!

The church was a poor village church; the whitewashed walls hung with the most primitive gaudy prints of the *Chemin de la Croix*, with here and there a humble *ex-voto*. Facing Vilpont was a rough painting of a stupendous black eye on a blue ground, symbolizing the ever-watchfulness of Providence. Few of the *cierges* being lighted, and ivy-branches trailing across the high, narrow windows, everything in the church was toned down to a soft gray, well calculated to promote tranquil, if not devotional, feeling. The nasal bass of the priest, the high, untutored trebles of the choir, the scraping of the fiddle, and the drone of the *serpent*, brought back a whole tide of recollections to Vilpont. Memory so smote on his heart, that his eyes filled with unwonted tears. He felt, as so many feel, that the acquisitions of manhood do not compensate for the hopes and faith of early youth.

Pauline saw—as women do see everything in any one who interests them—she saw that sudden filling of his eyes. How describe their effect upon her? In a second she had deified this man of the world. Her letters to Madame Agnes have shown the cravings of her young heart—have shown how her nature shrunk from the void of having no one to whom to give a woman's devotion. In this moment that void was filled by a joy that transfigured her sweet face. The period of crudeness and defiance, special to the girl who has never felt a preference, was about to vanish. With a new and vivid sensation she set aside her chair; and kneeling on the bare stone, her innocent soul associated this almost stranger with her inmost prayers.

As they were leaving the church a very old gentleman came forward—a thin, bent, white-haired man, dressed in a brown suit.

"My uncle Germain, my mother's eldest brother," said M. Jorey, presenting him to Vilpont.

"Uncle, will you come on the lake with us?" asked Stephanie.

"Very willingly, my child," he replied, in a feeble, quivering voice.

"A lake?" exclaimed Vilpont.

"Yes, sir, and worthy of your notice," replied the octogenarian with pride.

"Uncle, take care and bring the girls home in time for supper," said M. Jorey, lifting his hat, as he turned in another direction.

"Papa always has a long *tête-à-tête* with *bonne maman* on Sunday afternoon," explained Stephanie to Vilpont. "*Bonne maman* likes to hear all he has done during the week. She must have him all to herself, and then she pats his head and holds his hand in hers, just as she used to do when he was a child. 'He is still *my* boy,' she often says; and so mamma does not come till just before supper-time, and Uncle Germain takes care of us meanwhile."

Surely never was there a more fragile-looking guardian.

As they wound along the narrow, woodland path leading to the lake, by that double will which yet seems chance, Pauline and Vilpont came to be side by side.

Pauline at first frequently stopped to pick a flower, as though she thought nothing of her companion; but after two or three of these pretences of indifference, she succumbed to the new influence.

"What do you think of Uncle Germain?" she began.

"He is so bowed, so gentle-looking, yet so scarred by time, that I should imagine he had suffered a good deal."

Pauline said with a look of surprise, "How well you guess! but perhaps you have heard his story?"

"Not a word of it, I assure you."

"He is past eighty now, but when he was young he cared very much for a lady; she is still alive, and lives in St. Gloi. He was not rich enough, so she married some one else; and then about ten years afterwards her husband died, leaving her a great fortune.

Everybody expected that now she would marry Uncle Germain, for she had always declared she loved him."

"And I suppose they found out that they no longer cared for one another," interrupted Vilpont.

"He has never ceased to love her," said Pauline, with a slight vibration of indignation in her voice, "but *she* would not marry him; and they say"—here indignation sounded its full note—"they say she laughs at him. My mother suspects he knows it, and that it is that which makes him so sad-looking."

"My dear young lady, when you have lived longer you will discover how capricious human hearts are. Who knows whether, if the lady had proved kind, the gentleman would have remained constant?"

Pauline's eyes flashed on him as she replied, "If I am only to discover what is mean and bad, I do not wish to live."

Luckily just at this moment they emerged out of the chequered shade of the wood into the bright sunlight which set ablaze the yellow road and the greensward of the banks surrounding the lake—nothing in sight to mar the sylvan loveliness of the scene—a bird overhead letting fall sparse notes of song, some of the last he would sing that year—a gentle breeze just sufficient to make the high grass quiver—three nymph-like girls giving the life and coloring Poussin loved.

"Come away!" cried Julie from the boat,

3

unable to sympathize in Vilpont's admiration; "we are wasting precious time."

"Are you really going to row?" asked Vilpont, as he saw Pauline and Julie handling the oars.

"That's the pleasure of it," said Julie. "Uncle Germain will steer. Monsieur Vilpont, you and Stephanie are our passengers."

Vilpont took his seat according to orders, and away they went skimming over the unrippled waters. So calm was it, so vivid the reflection of the cloudless heaven, that they seemed to be gliding over a blue sky, behind them the trees, wrapped in violet mist.

After a little whispering among themselves, the girls began to sing "Adeste Fideles," the two rowing keeping time with their oars. On and on they passed, out of the bright light into where the lake, narrowing between two banks, was darkened by trees advancing to their edge. They stopped, and Stephanie said, "Now we must go home; it's my turn," and she took Pauline's oar.

"I wish there was no going back," said Vilpont.

"And the gigot and the bonbons!" cried out Julie.

"Ah! true, I had forgotten reality."

"But reality must not be forgotten," said Stephanie in her most dogmatic tone, "or we shall get among the osiers, and have a scolding into the bargain."

"You are right, mademoiselle; forgetting reality never fails to land one in a scrape. But common-sense need not prevent your singing again."

"As Pauline is not rowing, let her sing something alone."

"What shall it be?" asked Pauline.

"Uncle Germain's favorite—'Demain.'"

Leaning over the side, trailing one hand in the water as a sort of accompaniment, Pauline sang Madame Blanchecotte's pretty words set to music by the organist of St. Gloi—

> "Lon, lon la! les jours se passent
> Vides, misérablement!
> Lon, lon la! les cœurs se lassent
> D'errer éternellement!
> Toujours la même folie,
> Les mêmes tristes amours,
> Et toujours la même lie!
> Lon, lon la! toujours! toujours!
>
> "Lon, lon la! comme on se leurre
> D'être ferme et d'être fier!
> Lon, lon la! qu'on rie, qu'on pleure
> Demain recommence hier!
> Ou l'on est tombé l'on tombe!
> Nous ne cessons d'être fous
> Que les deux pieds sous la tombe;
> Lon, lon la! dessous! dessous!
>
> "Lon, lon la! d'un air de ronde
> Je voulais railler un peu
> Lon, lon la! ce pauvre monde,
> Si morose dans son jeu!
> Mais une angoisse subite
> Vint pleurer quand je chantais:
> De soi l'on n'est jamais quitte!
> Lon, lon la! jamais! jamais!"

Reader, have you ever listened to a happy child singing some ditty with sad words, the sadness of which it cannot comprehend, and not felt the pathos of the contrast between words and singer? This was what moved Vilpont to the very depth of his being, listening to such despairing words from the rosy lips of the fair girl before him — so unconscious of the struggles and anguish that informed the poet's lines.

With swift strokes they shot out of the gloom into long, glancing lines of light. The water had a voice also of its own—the breeze made a whispering among the trees; on went the boat with its freight of humanity—the sad old man on the verge of eternity, the disappointed man who had reached the "middle way of life," and three young creatures full of ardor and of belief that the world was a great storehouse of happiness.

Monsieur and Madame Rendu, with Madame Edmond Jorey, joined the supper-party. Madame Rendu looked far from pleased when she saw Vilpont, and made an opportunity to let him know that she never trusted Pauline alone to visit any one but her *marraine*.

The curé of the village was also there: he was treated like one of the family, and was evidently the confidant of the young girls. He had been their religious guide and instructor, and it was with him they had "made their first communion." It was pretty to see

how they waited on him, and how he entered
into all their jokes and playful ways.

The following morning, while De Saye and
his friend were smoking their cigars on the
terrace running along the front of Sept
Ormes, De Saye said :

" That busybody we dined with last week
told me that Mademoiselle Rendu's *dot* will
be only 200,000 francs (£8,000), and the
father and mother are only now middle-
aged."

Vilpont whistled.

" That's no answer," said De Saye, fret-
fully.

" The young lady herself has some value,"
replied Vilpont, dryly.

" She is agreeable enough, but the fortune
is preposterous ; only consider millinery ! My
sister finds six thousand francs too little for
her dress, and is always borrowing."

Vilpont puffed out a great cloud of smoke
before he replied :

" I'll tell you what, De Saye—win Mademoiselle Pauline if you can. She is superior
to the generality of girls, and believe me, my
good fellow, marriage is an excellent thing
when a man is young, and when he makes of
his wife the companion of his youth."

" If you have such a good opinion of Mademoiselle Pauline, why don't you propose for
her ? "

" I am too old, and—I am not worthy of
such a girl."

Yet Vilpont was, perhaps, better than ninety-nine out of a hundred of the men of his class. He might claim the superiority of having been made pretty often a dupe; further, that he was still able to believe in his fellow-beings, and was not like many of his associates, who paraded cynicism as a merit. He had, besides, talent that was nearly genius, and was without vanity. He was generous both in sentiment and deed; incapable of a meanness, as between man and man. With women his code of honor was less strict. He had not escaped the influences of his generation—of its prodigality, its discouragements, and its love of pleasure. One and all of these had left his mark on him.

When everything had been conjectured it was possible to conjecture about De Saye's antecedents, St. Gloi suddenly vibrated with curiosity as to who M. Vilpont was, and why he had come thither, and why he did not go away.

The Arch-priest's cook averred that Gonde had told her that never had she seen such linen as M. Vilpont's; it was a shame for a man, and a young man, to have such shirts; and everything else to match — brushes and combs fit for a prince. He was quiet enough in his ways; but there was a something about him which made Gonde suspect him.

"Suspect him of what?" asked the Arch-priest, full of alarm, lest Henri Rochefort had come among them in disguise.

Well, Gonde could not explain; but she was of opinion he was not what he seemed.

Little by little the curiosity of the St. Gloisians took a tinge of the fierceness of fear. The wish to know all your neighbor's concerns, and the habit of supposing evil unless you can gratify that desire for knowledge, are not peculiar to St. Gloi. Everywhere, save in great centres, or in places renowned for climate, folks require a patent reason for your coming among them. The bank-director's wife was the first to break ground. She one day said to Vilpont that he was the first person she had ever known who remained in St. Gloi without any obligation to do so.

"I am lazy," he answered. "I did not come willingly, but being here, I do not care to go. Are you anxious that I should?"

"Oh dear, no! only you must allow us to wonder a little."

"You mean to say that I am considered a suspicious character. Dear lady, I am nothing worse than a do-nothing, who, not being pressed by necessity, passes his days in busy idleness. I am without any nearer relation than an uncle and some distant cousins, who have no particular regard for me. If you have any reason for desiring my absence, I will be off to-morrow."

The lady colored and laughed as she disclaimed any such desire.

"To be candid with you," he went on, turning the lady into a warm partisan by this

semblance of confidence,—" To be candid
with you, nothing is more grateful to a man
tired of bustle and agitation, than a life where
one day resembles another. It is refreshing
to see the same faces, to listen to the same
conversations, over and over again; never to be
disturbed by hearing or seeing anything new.
It's a happiness, I assure you, merely to exist
where no one ventures to put forth an opinion. Paris, my usual home, becomes after a
time intolerable, with its never-ending theories, and its chase after novelty. The placid-
ity which reigns here, the shade of somno-
lence which prevails, is what I adore."

The listener was to the full as much puzzled
as flattered by this avowal. When she related
the conversation, as well as she could, to
Madame Rendu, that lady, with her practical
views, observed—

"Probably M. Vilpont meant what he said
about being sick of Paris. She had felt it
herself; and though it appeared he could do
without a profession, a long visit to Sept
Ormes might be a useful economy."

Once this opinion prevailed, Vilpont, in
spite of his fine linen, ceased to be an object
of alarm. Indeed, he lapsed into the category
of the unimportant, neither to be married by
Madame Chamband, nor reported of by the
sub-prefect to his chief.

## CHAPTER VII.

DISCOVERIES—ENDING WITH A CONFLAGRATION.

It was not long before it came to Pauline's ears that M. Vilpont had recommended M. de Saye to propose for her. Gonde, who from her kitchen windows had overheard part of the young man's conversation on the terrace, related in her own way what she had heard to the Arch-priest's cook; the Arch-priest's cook had given her version to the Joreys' ladies'-maid, and she again had retailed the gossip to the young ladies as they were going to bed.

The next morning Pauline was told by Stephanie and Julie, under the seal of the strictest confidence, that Vilpont and De Saye had cast lots which should marry her, and that De Saye had won; but he had objected that she dressed too extravagantly, and had offered to give her up to Vilpont, who had distinctly said no—she was too dangerous.

Pauline, though her face crimsoned painfully, was less shocked than an English girl would have been; she knew how often marriages were discussed in a bargaining spirit in France.

"Let us think of some way to punish them," said Stephanie.

3*

" But how can girls punish men ? " asked
the more timid Julie.

" Let us all agree never to dance with
either of them," was Stephanie's proposal.

" No such thing ; that would only make a
horrible talk through the town, and perhaps
turn the laugh against me," said Pauline.
" After all, *we* discuss them pretty freely, and
we should think M. Vilpont very absurd if he
resented my saying he was not so handsome
as his friend."

" But suppose M. de Saye proposes for you ? "

" I shall take his proposal into consideration."

" And if M. Vilpont were to come forward ? "

" I should answer precisely in the same
way. That is, however, not likely, as he calls
me dangerous."

" What could he mean ? " asked Julie.

" The very question I should put if he did
propose."

" And so you have given up your ideal ? "
said Stephanie.

" On the contrary, I never thought so much,
and so seriously, of him as at the present
moment."

" I cannot make you out, Pauline, you are
so changed."

" Am I ? " returned the young girl, running
to a glass.

" Yes," continued Stephanie ; " even your
face is changed."

"Tell me how and where, for I do not see it," said Pauline, pushing back her hair, and dropping on her knees before Stephanie. "Do you see any wrinkles?"

Stephanie looked long at the upturned face. "You don't care for us so much as you did—I know it, I see it."

"Little goose! there never was a time I loved you so much. When I think that perhaps next year, even in a few months, we may all be separated, that we may be at the different ends of France, that all these good talks may be over forever and ever, that we may be sick and sorry among strangers, I am ready to cry." Here she jumped up, and exclaimed, "Suppose we all three go to the Curé and take a solemn oath never to marry, always to live together."

"Mamma would never forgive us," murmured Julie.

"The Curé would not let us," said Stephanie; "besides, every one marries."

"Then let us talk of something else," rejoined Pauline, a little ashamed of herself, as we all are when cold water is thrown on our enthusiasm.

Nowhere is there less liberty to do as you please than in small towns. Unless you wish to offer up your reputation and your person as food for idle comment, you must learn to put a restraint on all your looks, words, and actions; even to take care of your thoughts. You must do as others do, have no aims higher

than theirs. You may strive to be rich, to
marry your sons and daughters to the best advantage, keeping your daughters strictly under
a veil as impenetrable as that of Isis; but be-
ware of generosity, or of enthusiasm, or of
strong convictions. Creep, creep along the
smooth, beaten path of mediocrity, and you
will meet your reward—you will be trusted
and respected.

Vilpont was once more becoming both
dreaded and despised. The discovery had
been made that he was an author. St. Gloi
feared the uncommon, feared all that did not
run on beaten paths. An author had never
been seen in St. Gloi. Vilpont was regarded
as an incorporation of Dr. Faustus and the
devil, and looked upon with a curious mixture
of contempt and awe.

De Saye came in for his share of blame for
introducing this writer of plays into "the
society;" but then every one excused him because he was unmarried, and could not be expected to be so careful as to his associates as
he would be by and by. The matrons of St.
Gloi had pitiful hearts, as most matrons have,
for a good *parti*. So, though treated with
additional reserve, Vilpont was not yet
avoided.

Two or three of the most adventurous
spirits, indeed, had a secret desire to see what
he had written, but they dared not breathe
aloud that desire. The stupidest of the *crème
de la crème* nicknamed him *Le beau ténébreux*

—an epithet picked out of some newspaper story.

Only old Madame Jorey supported Vilpont. He had returned more than once to visit the lake, and each time had called at the château and had a long chat with *bonne maman*.

Even these walks were a subject for suspicion. The St. Gloisians looked on woods and valleys merely in the light of investments—none understood disinterested admiration for the country—none among them, indeed, could have found their way through the forests encircling St. Gloi. Were there not railways to any place which it was necessary to visit? So the topography of the department was generally ignored by what are called the "better classes."

Madame Jorey stood her ground against her daughters-in-law, who were among the fiercest alarmists. The old lady declared she had seen men enough in her life to know an honest one from a rogue; and though she would not answer for M. Vilpont as a saint, she would guarantee his being a *galant homme*.

Matters were in this dubious state, when, for the first time since Gonde's gossip had reached her, Pauline and Vilpont met at an evening party given by Madame Chambaud.

That lady, still on projects of matrimony intent, had prudently kept herself neutral as regarded Vilpont. How could she invite M. de Saye and not his friend? and how promote a preference in M. de Saye for Pauline if he never met her? So Vilpont, still unconscious of his unpopularity, appeared, with his usual air of indifference, in Madame Chambaud's *salon*. He did not even remark a studied coldness in the manner his bows were received. What he did observe was a defiant sparkle in Pauline's eyes when they met his. She, poor child, was indifferent as to his being an author. What she did smart under was his supposed expressed disapprobation and indifference. She had intended to make no change in her manner towards him; but it is difficult, even for the most wary, to hide a strong impression, a hope, or a doubt. So Vilpont perceived at once that she had no longer any friendly feeling for him, and wondered what could be the cause of the change. He was leagues away from any right guess.

These two people were equally preoccupied by one another, and equally desirous not to show that preoccupation—Vilpont, from experience of the sharpness of provincial eyes; Pauline, from womanly instinct.

Nevertheless, an irresistible attraction was drawing them together. Pauline struggled against it, keeping herself well within a group of girls, talking, whispering, laughing, notwithstanding many grave, rebuking looks from Madame Rendu, or an occasional reproachful " Allons, donc mesdemoiselles " from other mothers.

" What a child Pauline still is ! " murmured Madame Chambaud.

"Too much so, madame," was the severe re-joinder.

Madame Chambaud's request for the usual dose of music had been met by so universal a pleading for the cotillon, that she had yielded to the popular voice.

M. de Saye and Madame Gréemard were elected as leaders.

Vilpont, saying he had long given up dancing, took a seat by Madame Rendu. He had a secret wish to propitiate her.

"A poor exhibition for you, monsieur," was how she began *her* attack. "A poor exhibition for you, who are accustomed to Paris and the ballet."

"This is a far prettier sight, madame, than a ballet—as superior as fresh flowers are to artificial ones."

"Monsieur is very polite."

"And with perfect sincerity, madame."

Vilpont was watching Pauline. One of the prettiest figures of the cotillon is that in which the cavalier carries a net to catch the butterfly the lady waves before him, fixed on the end of a flexible wand. M. de Saye was the pursuer, and Pauline the defender. Vilpont was really justified in his admiration—so swiftly, so gracefully did the girl bend and elude all attacks. It was evident to him that her defence was in earnest. The struggle was so prolonged that the lookers-on grew interested, and stood up to see the result. De Saye, so noted a cotillon hero, was piqued by such res-

olute resistance, and put forth all his strength
and dexterity, using his advantages of height
and length of arm. More than once the butterfly escaped capture but by a hair's-breadth ;
until, when so sorely pressed that defeat
seemed certain, a flash of fire sparkled on the
end of the wand. With a cry of dismay the
dancers dispersed. The butterfly had caught
fire at one of the candles of the chandelier—
whether by accident or design, Pauline kept
to herself. With a low curtsey to M. de Saye,
she went to her mother's side.

"Permit me to offer you my compliments,
mademoiselle, on your graceful and successful
defence," said Vilpont.

"I do not approve of playing with fire," observed Madame Rendu, not at all pleased.
"Why," thought she, "could not Pauline manage to be more like other girls?"

"I am sorry for the butterfly ; it was very
pretty," said Pauline.

Madame Rendu was obliged at this moment
to listen to a long-winded oration from the
pedantic young Juge d'Instruction.

Vilpont, standing behind Pauline, said in a
low voice—

"You burned the butterfly on purpose."

"O monsieur! do not give yourself the
trouble to explain a little girl's whims. They
are often silly, but never dangerous."

All the evening Pauline had been meditating how, in speaking, she could manage to
bring in that offending word. She had laid

more emphasis on it than she was conscious of doing, and, though she did her best to look unconscious, Vilpont felt that there was more meant than met the ear.

"Is that a riddle for me to guess?" and he fixed her eyes firmly with his own. It was hawk and jenny-wren.

There was a passing little quiver of the girl's lips, which tacitly invoked his mercy; but otherwise she did not quail, and said proudly—

"You have no right to suppose anything about me!"

"I beg you a thousand pardons, mademoiselle." And he left her.

Pauline went to bed that night believing that she was glad she had offended M. Vilpont.

As M. de Saye and Vilpont went home, Gaston said—

"Let us walk quick. That cotillon was as bad as a vapor-bath."

"Mademoiselle Pauline is as nimble as a squirrel," returned Vilpont.

"Not so nimble but that I could have caught her but for that stupid accident."

"Ah! yes. How did she manage it—so little as she is?"

"Manage it! You don't suppose she did it on purpose?"

"I suspect so. And I retract the advice I gave you about her."

"A girl's coquetry need be no scarecrow."

"As you please."

"Perhaps you are thinking of her for yourself?"

"Were I as good a fellow as I was at twenty-five, and with all the money I have squandered in the meantime, I should try my luck. How she came to be the child of that father and mother is a miracle; unless, indeed, it is a case of reversion, such as Darwin mentions, to the merits of some remote and exceptional ancestor. No; I am not thinking of her for myself. Life is for her yet a fairy tale, full of light and joy; mine is like a modern ruin. Besides, I am about to bid you goodby. To-morrow I begin my farewell visits."

"Going already?" exclaimed De Saye, striving after a tone of regret.

"Already?" repeated Vilpont laughing; "don't be severe on my tardiness."

De Saye grumbled some words in his beard.

"I am off to Homburg, or Baden-Baden, or some other place of Satanic gathering," added Vilpont.

# CHAPTER VIII.

## WHO WAS LAST NOW FIRST.

VILPONT sowed his cards of adieu liberally
through the town; he neglected no one with
whom he had even exchanged a bow. He was
admitted at the Rendus. Madame (who was
alone) had never been so nearly civil to him as
when she heard he was going away directly;
and yet, though pleased that this man, who
had no business in St. Gloi, should go, she
could not help saying, in a tone of pique, that
" he must have made a great sacrifice to friendship in staying so long in so dull a place."

Vilpont, determined that he would not allow
her to ride over him as she did every one,
answered in a lofty way, which had its effect
on her—

"My dear lady, we are no judges of one
another's sacrifices, the best of which often remain unknown."

He then thanked her for the hospitality shown
to a stranger, and, with his *hommages empresses*
for Mademoiselle Pauline, bowed himself out
of the room in a manner unattainable by any
but a Frenchman born.

At dinner Vilpont mentioned rather em-
phatically that he had paid his visit to the
Rendus, but had not seen Mademoiselle
Pauline. He laughed at the stiffness with

which he had been received everywhere, and ended by fixing to leave the day after the next. He should devote the following morning to old Madame Jorey, the only person who had really been cordial to him.

De Saye had recovered his good-humor, and was even more than usually demonstrative. Eloque had a petrified grin on his face as he obeyed the order to bring St. Peray and Château Margaux. He nudged Gonde when he went down to fetch the wine.

"How he loves his friend! how sorry he is that he is going!"

"Old bear!" returned Gonde; then to herself, "Why does he go? he has had no letter. He did not mean it three days ago, for he said nothing about his linen from the wash."

The friends had promised to spend the evening at the bank-director's. To their surprise, they found quite a large party assembled. A Madame d'Allot and her young daughter had arrived quite unexpectedly, and as unexpectedly the young secretary of the prefect had come on an official errand to the bank-director.

Madame Perrotier had at once sent to invite the Rendus and Chambauds for the evening.

Madame d'Allot was a true Parisian—lively eyes, fine hair, a ravishing toilette, pretty, without one pretty feature. The daughter, yet a mere child, a nice little puppet, that answered well as a chaperone.

Never had Vilpont received such a flatter-

ing welcome in St. Gloi. He wondered at
first if he owed this cordiality to the knowledge that he was going away. But he soon
found that he was indebted to Madame
d'Allot, who had been enlightening the company as to M. Vilpont's importance in Paris.
She had told them, in wittily covert terms,
that they had been contemning. Apollo, and
assuredly he would send some of his arrows to
punish them.

Half mystified and half regretful were the
feelings of her listeners. Madame d'Allot
herself had neither eyes nor ears for any one
but Vilpont. The young secretary, type of all
Cherubinos past and future, was instructing
Pauline as to Vilpont's fame and genius. As
the two young heads leaned toward one
another, Madame d'Allot said in a loud whisper—

"What a pretty picture!—subject for an
idyl."

"Ancient history for me," laughed Vilpont.

Presently the young secretary, who was by
no means troubled with bashfulness, said to
Madame Perottier—

"If it would afford you pleasure, madame, I
should be happy to recite some pages of M.
Vilpont's most celebrated poems."

The proposition was, with some trepidation,
accepted. Vilpont made no objection, simply
begging to be allowed to sit in a corner.

Cherubino assumed an appropriate pose.

He recited well what was in truth a touching story told in beautiful verse.

Vilpont, from his refuge, had a view of Pauline. He saw her gradually slip behind the curtain of the window near which she sat. Could he doubt it was done to conceal her emotion?

The poem, perhaps, took up half an hour, and was concluded amid a clapping of hands and application of embroidered handkerchiefs to the ladies' eyes. Vilpont was complimented in all keys. Pauline remained hiding behind the curtain. He drew nearer and nearer to her. He saw that she looked grave. To his dismay, he heard her say to Cherubino—

"Oh! forgive me, but it was so long, it sent me to sleep. Poetry always does."

For the nonce Vilpont felt that Pauline was as unsuited to him as he to her. He told the story to De Saye with much humor.

"It is charming," he said, "to be innocent, but not too innocent—of nothing too much."

The following morning he set off to bid old Madame Jorey good-by. He was eager to leave St. Gloi. The only creature in it who had interested him had turned out a disappointment. His imagination had invented a Pauline quite different from the real one. He wished her well—a good bourgeois husband with plenty of money and very little wit. The whole length of the walk, Pauline occupied his thought. He was angry with her— what right had she to be stupid, with that face

so full of animation? And he had thought
her too good to be the child of the Rendus!
Pauline had thoroughly avenged the offence
reported by Gonde.

In this mood Vilpont reached Château Ste.
Marie. It is perfectly unlike an English
country-house, or indeed any sort of English
house. It is a large, bare, white building, the
white turned green and mouldy at all the
corners, and round the windows. It stands on
a slight rise in the middle of a paddock parched
to a brown yellow at that moment. All the
beauty of the place lies away among the hills
sheltering the lake.

Madame Jorey cared nothing for scenery,
and a great deal for her vineyards on the Côtes
Ste. Marie, these *côtes* being sharply steep hills
divided from each other by deep gorges, which
every year are ploughed deeper and deeper by
mountain torrents. *Bonne maman* was an
excellent woman of business, as indeed French-
women generally are; probably the result of
the equal division of property. As a rule,
there is not much helplessness among women
in France; they have more common-sense and
less imagination than their sisters in neighboring countries.

Vilpont found *bonne maman* in her morning dress, a lose print jacket and dimity petticoat, her gray hair twisted up in brown-paper
*papillotes*, and busy with a cooper, inspecting
empty wine-barrels. She welcomed her visitor without any embarrassment; sent him

into the house, promising to join him in a quarter of an hour, when the twelve o'clock breakfast would be ready.

Vilpont did as he was bid, making friends with one of the fat maids to get the dust taken off his outer man, and then made himself comfortable on the one sofa in the room, a sofa large enough, however, to make three modern ones. He did what all people do who write—observe, compare, and reflect when in a strange place. He noticed the complete absence of any signs of refinement; indeed, a stranger to the country might have mistaken such scantiness and coarseness in the curtains, such absence of carpets, such hardness and diminutiveness in the chairs, as signs of smallness of means. But all these things were but the outward signs of the character and habits of their owner. Madame Jorcy was yet near enough to her peasant ancestors to love hoarding for hoarding's sake. As long as she had good strong chairs to sit on, a good bed to lie on, and plenty to put on her deal table, she was satisfied. Her eyes, as she declared, did not require to be feasting on silks and velvets. She was one of those penetrated by the wisdom of saving sous. She shrunk from the fact of parting with coin, but not with coin's worth. She was liberal to her poor neighbors with milk and wine and flour, wilfully blind to the bundles of brushwood gleaned in her woods; but ask her for money, and she lost her temper. She did her visitor the honor of taking her hair out of paper before sitting down to table.

The breakfast, though served on common ware, was excellent. Vilpont said no better could have been had in Paris.

"Paris!" exclaimed the old lady; "you never got such cream, or eggs, or bread in Paris. Don't talk to me about Paris. Stay to dinner, and see if Nanette doesn't beat your Paris."

Vilpont told her that his visit was a farewell one—he was to be off the next day.

"Where are you going?"

"First to Baden-Baden—"

"You would do much better to stay away. What's taking you there?"

"Idleness, and, principally, want of a home."

"Poor fellow!—why don't you marry?"

He made a grimace.

"That's nonsense," she said; "don't tell me. You are not of the sort that don't like women, or that women don't like. I can judge, though I am a grandmother, a man of your age ought to be married, and have some little, brown brats creeping about his knees. That's better than running after powder-faced dolls, who have as little heart as beauty."

"My dear lady, I am not rich enough to marry; and I have besides a decided objection to our French system of marriage."

"You're wrong, altogether wrong. I married my husband after seeing him twice, and I did very well. My sons married the girls I

4

chose for them, and their households are happy
ones. Now, listen to me, my friend: when
folks marry for love, they begin with a whole
batch of illusions, which day by day vanish, and
often the once loving pair come cordially to
hate one another—I have seen it. But when
parents make the choice, they do so with all
their reason; they look out for good health,
good antecedents—a great deal in antecedents;
good conduct runs in the blood, so does bad.
If a woman behaves well, and makes a house
comfortable, the man comes to value her; and
as soon as he does that, she loves him. Women
are made so—they give a great deal for very
little."

"Suppose I agree with your theory, what
then? I have no parents to choose a wife for
me; my only near relation, and uncle in Bretagne, hates my very name, because I refuse
to bury myself with him and his prejudices;
and then, as I have had the pleasure of telling
you, I am poor, and have a decided horror of
heiresses."

"H'm—how do you manage to live?"

"As you already know, by writing plays and
story-books."

The good lady said rapidly, "Tiens, tiens,
tiens, tiens!"—just as an Englishwoman would
have exclaimed, "Dear, dear me!"

"And you can live by that?"

"Tolerably."

"Now will you satisfy an old woman's curiosity. How much do you gain?"

He took out a pocket-book.—"My author's rights on my last comedy brought me in eighteen months twenty thousand francs; that is all spent. Good year and bad year, we may reckon that I make from twenty-five to thirty thousand francs; and with the interest of a small patrimony, I sometimes manage to get through the year without heavy debts."

*Bonne maman* stared at him with open mouth.

"You are not telling me fairy tales?"

"On my word of honor."

"Well, that a man can make all that money by a parcel of lies does make my gray hair bristle up."

Vilpont laughed, saying, "There is often more truth in comedy than in history."

She shook her head, and said, "I am afraid you are right not to marry, for I suppose you live among those theatre-people."

"Of course, I see a great deal of them; I have to dance attendance on the lady who acts my heroine, to study her style of beauty, her humors, even occasionally to fancy myself in love with her, and make her fancy it also."

"*Fripon*, hold your tongue! don't talk to a decent grandmother of such doings! I give you up."

"That is the bad result of my sincerity."

"You cannot hope," she said, "that I should recommend any nice girl to marry you."

"Such a hope is the furthest from my thoughts. I am quite aware that my past is

to be the executioner of my future. I begin
to understand now the coldness with which I
have been lately treated by my St. Gloi acquaintances, and believe me when I say you
are the only one I quit with regret."

"Ah, you serpent beguiling my ears! But
I am not going to let you off so easily. My
sons and their families are away to see after
their own vintage, so there's no danger in that
quarter. You want looking after; you are a
mere bag of bones. I expect to hear them
rattle as you walk. Come and stay a week in
this good air and get strong, for your horrible
Baden. I'll give you a room looking to the
west, where you can write your poetry, for I
never need company during the day—there's
something in that yellow face of yours I like
—and in the evening you can tell me more
about your life."

"You are very kind."

"That's what I mean to be. So you'll stay.
I'll send for your clothes, and you can write
to your friend not to expect you back yet
awhile."

# CHAPTER IX.

## A LILIPUTIAN VENGEANCE.

ACCORDING as chance places people, so do they show different sides of themselves. We know that it is so by the various judgments passed on the same individuals by their acquaintances. Approval in country towns is most generally allotted to those who never buffet against the current, who accept routine as the surest of guides. De Saye was one of this type ; Vilpont of that other, which chooses an eccentric orbit. The appellation of " Lion " figures forth the feeling excited in obscure places by unusual talents.

Vilpont was considered decidedly unpleasant by the St. Gloisians ; they were pleased to hear of his departure.

Madame Jorey (though she did not make it known) had a decided admiration for him, ripening into a real liking. She was reckoned by her daughters-in-law and their set as uncouth and stupid. Vilpont found her shrewd, with quick perceptions and an affectionate disposition. The man of letters and the woman of none passed a cheerful evening together ; indeed, Vilpont had not been once so pleasant during the couple of months he had spent in St. Gloi, as he was during this after-dinner chat. His very face seemed changed.

"You look younger already than you did this morning," observed Madame Jorey. "How old are you?"

"My thirty-third birthday is close at hand."

"I took you for older. I shall marry you yet."

"What a pity you are not yourself five-and-twenty years younger, madame."

"Ah! lad, a fine couple we should have made—fire and water. I should have done my best, I can tell you, to put out your fire. I could never have abided your actresses."

"I will tell you something that will surprise you: I have never been in love yet."

"Ta—ta—ta!—you expect an old woman like me to believe you. I know your sex better; from the time they put on their collegian's uniform they are always in love, the little rascals. When I was six, I had a love-letter from a boy of eight."

"Allowed; but I am speaking of some very different feeling—one that would send a man to Kamschatka or bring him back at a woman's will."

"One of your monstrous theatrical lies! And how long do you think you would care for that same woman? As soon as she belonged to you, you would be for sending her to Kamschatka, and not bringing her back. I thought you had more sense."

The next day Vilpont wandered to the lake. As he rested under the shade of the trees, the scene of the girls in the boat, the withered old man, living or rather dying in his illusions, the previous pretty picture of the bonbon-making, all returned in force to his memory, suggesting the groundwork of a new poem. He was roused from a deep reverie by a shrill shout. Looking up, he saw his dream realized. Pauline Rendu was rowing towards him. As the boat approached the shore, he saw that her companions were not the Mesdemoiselles Jorey, but Madame d'Allot and her young daughter.

"Madame Jorey sent us in search of you," screamed little Mademoiselle d'Allot at the top of her voice.

Pauline looked flushed with her exertions.

Madame d'Allot insisted on getting out of the boat just where Vilpont was now standing, in spite of Pauline's telling her that the usual landing-place was not twenty yards distant. No; Madame d'Allot could jump ashore if M. Vilpont would promise to catch her, which M. Vilpont agreed to do with the eagerness incumbent on him to show.

"If you let me drop, I shall never forgive you," said the lady, balancing herself on the stern of the boat in an attitude that reminded Vilpont of a heroine of melodrama.

"Steady, Mademoiselle Pauline!" he cried out, and Mademoiselle Pauline kept her oars quiet, with an expression of profound disgust on her face.

"One, two, three!" and the lady sprung into the arms of the gentleman, who held her in as tight a clasp as she could desire before setting her Cinderella feet on the ground.

"Now Alix," cried the widow to her daughter.

"Thank you, mamma; I am fat and afraid."

Off went the boat with rapid strokes. Madame d'Allot cried out—

"But my daughter—come, come!"

"Adieu, adieu!" chorused the two girls, as the boat glided away.

"It is a bad trick," said Madame d'Allot.

Vilpont was waving his hat and laughing. Pauline bid Alix wave her handkerchief in return. The boy steering grinned with delight.

"We have a long walk before us, madame; for we must go round the lake to reach the Château."

"What a spiteful girl! None but a provincial would have behaved so rudely; and Alix—suppose she is drowned!"

Madame d'Allot was frightened as well as angry; and she hated walking, particularly in those lovely tight boots.

"Mademoiselle Alix is safe," said Vilpont; "the boat is made so that it cannot upset, and we can take it leisurely. Do you grudge me this pleasure—the greater for being unexpected; so long since any such came in my way," etc., etc.

Vilpont knew the part he had to play, and did it unexceptionably.

Madame d'Allot liked admiration and flirt-

ing as well as most of her compeers, but she
was not sentimentally given; she made excur-
sions into the *pays de tendre* simply as a pas-
time. She skimmed along its frontiers with
men, just as she talked millinery with her
milliner.

So, leaning on Vilpont's arm, now meeting,
now avoiding his admiring gaze, in the most
approved fashion, she let him know that St.
Gloi was in convulsions of curiosity to find
out why he had chosen to leave M. de Saye
to have a *tête-à-tête* with *cette vieille ménagère*.
M. de Saye had smiled, shrugged his shoulders,
and called it a poetical license.

"To save your reputation, monsieur," she
went on, "I coaxed that bunch of thorns,
Madame Rendu, to drive me here (a work of
charity, you understand), that I might tranquil-
lize the minds of the St. Gloisians."

"A good, beautiful fairy! Are you tired?
Shall we rest?"

"No. We must not give that dreadful girl
too much time to tell her story; but now, do
explain why you bury yourself here."

"Simple as two and two make four. Madame Jorey desired me to stay, and I stayed.
I never know how to say no to a woman,
whatever her age. I am a perfect slave to any
of the dear sex who shows me kindness."

"Men are are not in general noted for gratitude."

"How strangely women ignore our natures.
Madame Jorey says just as you do. Now, I

4*

take all my gods to witness that I am like melted wax to kindness. With me love begets love; I could not love where there was no response."

"How often have you made the experiment?"

"Several times. Once, indeed, I was nearly attaching myself like a limpet to a rock, when, luckily or unluckily, I received a note in which *cœur* was spelled *cure*. I tried to pardon the offence—in vain. Ah! dear lady, I have more memories of painful liberations than of happy captivities. I have sung my dream in the emptiness of many a heart." *

"It's so easy for a man to say he has suffered—so difficult to make sure of it," said the lady, beginning to feel sorry she had taken the trouble to look after Vilpont.

During this time the boat, though still in sight, was speeding away from the couple; all at once, however, they saw it turn and make towards them.

"I hate that girl Rendu," said Madame d'Allot; "she looks as innocent as milk, and she is as sharp as vinegar."

"We must receive the repentant sinner with joy," said Vilpont; "particularly as her return will save fatigue to those lovely little feet, never meant to tread rough roads."

Pauline was in truth repenting her escapade, and rather alarmed for its consequences.

* "J'ai fait chanter mon rêve au vide de ton cœur."— *Corneille.*

Madame d'Allot made no remark until she was again safely seated on the boat-cushions. Vilpont had asked and obtained a place, and now took an oar to assist Pauline.

"Pray, young ladies," began Madame d'Allot, "will you give us some explanation of your conduct."

"Don't be angry, mamma, dear," said the fat Alice, smoothing down her mother's arm with her little red fingers. "Pauline said she was afraid to stay alone in the boat, and she could not jump because of her ugly boots."

"Vanity is always a bad counsellor, mademoiselle," said Vilpont, with great gravity.

"Yes, monsieur," was the reply, with a demure look.

When they were landing, Pauline said to Madame d'Allot:

"Be so very good, madame, as not to complain of me. My mother would be very angry if she knew how rude I have been—and I beg your pardon."

"It is not worth speaking about, mademoiselle," returned the lady dryly.

Pauline kept entirely in the background during the whole evening, often hid from sight behind her godmother's broad back,

When they were all gone, Madame Jorey said to Vilpont—

"My god-daughter is a jewel of a girl. Could any man look in her face, and fear to take her on trust?"

"The surface is very fair," he replied;

"but what woman's looks can be trusted? My trade makes me an observer of trifles; and from one or two little incidents that have occurred, I infer Mademoiselle Pauline is something quick-tempered."

"What is that you tell me?" exclaimed Madame Jorey, starting up and standing before him, one arm akimbo. "Pauline quick-tempered? Why, Mr. Author, she is just clear sunshine, making all things bright and pleasant. Neither father nor mother are saints—*pardi;*—why, they would drive such as I am mad. Madame so sharp and suspicious; he so full of his fidgets and his terrors about this and that; and yet that little girl manages to make them endurable, sweetens her mother, and heartens up her father. People hated to go near them till she came; and as for a heart, why there's not a soul in trouble but goes to Pauline Rendu. She's not squeamish, makes no pretence of not knowing that there's evil in the world. I shan't tell you what she made me do, because perhaps you might think she had better have kept her eyes and ears shut. Pauline bad-tempered! You should not have her if you begged on your knees for a month."

"She would be quite of your way of thinking, dear madame; but hear the reasons, at least one of them, for the accusation," and Vilpont related how Pauline had deserted Madame d'Allot.

"The little rogue!" and Madame Jorey chuckled.

"Fine gentleman and fine lady left in the lurch. And so that's why she hid behind me, and didn't bid me invite them all for Sunday; but I'll have her, and make her speak out for herself. Pauline bad-tempered! Why, even when she was teething, she was as good as a *petit St. Jean*. And now, my clever sir, read me some of that," and she held out his own last poem, the one recited by Cherubino.

"How did you come by it?" he asked.

"Read, and let me judge of what gains you your daily bread."

He hesitated.

"Perhaps you fancy I am not able to understand it," said the old lady a little nettled. "If it's good, it will go to every heart. Didn't our greatest man trust to an old servant-woman's judgment?"

"Suppose I dread your judgment."

She shrugged her shoulders. "Are you satisfied yourself?"

"No."

"Very well. Now, let me hear."

Never before had Vilpont felt so timid. That clear-headed, honest-hearted woman would never swallow any sentimental clothing of evil, and he could recollect many sentences which were sophistical arguments to prove wrong right and right wrong. However, he must undergo the ordeal, or offend his new friend. He gained courage as he read. Not one musical phrase, not one true sentiment, but she showed she thoroughly appreciated.

She even shed some few tears, for which he almost stopped to thank her. The dubious passages she groaned loudly over; but when he had finished, she called out, "Embrassez-moi, mon garçon!" and without waiting to be obeyed, gave him a sounding kiss on each cheek.

"There's good, great good in you," she went on. "Ah! if you had only a dear little wife, and two brown-faced boys at your knees."

"Amen!" he said.

# CHAPTER X.

## THE IDEAL.

On Sunday, the Rendu *calèche* brought the father, mother, Pauline, and little Alix d'Allot to Ste. Marie. They arrived before ten o'clock, as they meant all to go and attend mass at the village church.

Pauline was not so rosy as usual; her manner, too, was tinged by a new shyness and reserve. The greater delicacy of her complexion made her more than ever like one of Greuze's delicious portraits of girls. As she walked with her tripping step by her mother's side, her dainty, well-poised, small figure showing to admiration in the blue muslin gown, stirred—only just stirred—by the gentle, autumn breeze, a man must have had his heart well defended to have kept her out of it.

Their road lay through an avenue of lime-trees, glorious in foliage, and full of murmurings; the sun, striking through every opening of branch and twig, seemed to bar the path with long trembling lines of light.

Pauline, who had begun by walking decorously before reaching the end of the avenue, had not resisted the temptation to skip over these luminous barriers. Once, after doing this, she turned, forced by some mysterious attraction, towards Vilpont. Perhaps he was not himself aware of the tenderness and admiration of his eyes.    Pauline, catching the look, flushed, and moved hastily on, so that all he could see of her face was one crimsoned ear, like some small, transparent shell.    She turned no more ; nor could he do more than occasionally get a glimpse of her in the church, she having placed herself between her mother and *bonne maman.*

He waited for her in the porch, and as she came out, said—

"Allow me, mademoiselle, to carry your book."

She gave it him at once.    Curious little ways girls have of showing a preference.

He, on his side, resisted a strong inclination to put the book to his lips.    He remembered in time that he was in the midst of a country congregation, to whom all the doings of their betters were matters of intensest interest, and only buttoned his coat over it.    He cherished it there almost as if he had held on his breast the pretty hand of its owner.    As for Pauline, her young heart was beating with a feeling that paled her cheek and softened her eyes. Was it wrong to have given the book to M. Vilpont?    Ought she to tell her mother *all* about it?

The Rendus knew almost every one at Ste. Marie, and the salutations to be exchanged were endless.    There were the *maire* and the schoolmaster to be spoken to, and the important dame who took care of the dear old Curé.

During these ceremonies Pauline recovered her composure. At last M. le Curé himself appeared, and joining Madame Jorey, she leading, they proceeded to the Château. Vilpont walked with M. Rendu; he had made no effort further to approach Pauline. All at once she seemed too far removed from him—too superior to allow of his treating her as he might the other mesdames and mesdemoiselles of his acquaintance. He walked with her father, and tried to listen to his platitudes. Such platitudes! it was a marvel how small a man's mind could be.

Once, when Vilpont awoke out of a reverie, he found M. Rendu in the middle of a story as to how he had discovered that Madame une Telle used a depilatory powder to destroy a nascent moustache. And this man was Pauline's father. His former opinion that she was a bird of paradise had revived.

As they entered the hall, Madame Rendu's high voice was heard asking, " Pauline, where is thy book? I do not see it—thy grandmother's present."

Vilpont, extricating it dexterously from its place of concealment, returned it to the young lady.

" No harm, no harm," said Madame Jorey— " a piece of Paris politeness." And Vilpont could hear her whispering to Madame Rendu, " A good fellow—very good."

The Curé's place at the mid-day Sunday dinner was always on one side of his hostess,

and on his other side was now Pauline, whom
he had christened and confirmed, and whom
he hoped to marry happily.

Vilpont sat by Madame Rendu, and the
*vicaire* (curate) had charge of little Mademoiselle d'Allot, who was made silent by amazement at the company she found herself among.
The *maire*, the schoolmaster also, regular
Sunday guests with M. Rendu, filled the other
seats.

Pauline recovered her gayety under the wing
of M. le Curé. She played him all sorts of
girlish tricks: stole his bread, kidnapped his
napkin, pulled crackers with him, inducing him
to read mottoes out of keeping with his calling.

"Do you mean always to be a child, Pauline?" asked Madame Rendu with more gen-
tleness in her tone than was usual.

"I shall forgive her everything if she speaks
thus to her child," thought Vilpont, saying
aloud, "Who could wish for any change in
her?"

"As for that," said the lady with her wonted
sharpness, "she is neither better nor worse than
others;" adding, "We ought to be very much
flattered by a gentleman so famous as I hear
you are, lingering here. You must not, however, be offended if we wonder why you do so."

To this plain speaking, on which Madame
Rendu prided herself, he replied—

"No doubt, in your varied reading, madame,
you have met with a description of a certain
plant which deprives all those who eat of it of

any desire for change. Place but a leaf between your teeth, you will forget everything you once cared for—you will stay where you are, leading a sort of dormouse-life, unless carried away by main force. That is my present condition."

The Curé, who had overheard this sally, said—

"The wise man refused to eat of that plant, Monsieur Vilpont."

"You see, madame, that M. le Curé guarantees the truth of my story."

"I don't care for men's stories; they are seldom fit for women's ears," snapped out Madame Rendu.

"Not even such a girl as Pauline could make amends for such a mother," thought Vilpont, and as soon as they rose from table went away for a long, solitary walk, his usual remedy for ruffled temper.

His thoughts, however, were full of Pauline; all day De Musset's description of an Englishwoman had been running in his head—

> "Elle était simple et bonne,
> Ne sachant pas le mal, elle faisait le bien.
> Des richesses du cœur elle me fit l'aumône ;
> Sans oser y penser, je donnai le mien.
> Elle emporta ma vie, et n'en sut jamais rien."

He meant now more than ever that she should know nothing of the tenderness she had awakened in his heart. He classed her among those unknown oppressed of the earth whose delicate natures are doomed to suffer from the

ignorance, insipidity, narrow-mindedness that
surround them. She would be the victim of
the passionate personality, the prejudices incar-
nate in her mother, and of the weakness of her
father; he foresaw all the deceptions and disappointments life had in store for her. Running on, side by side with these thoughts of
her, was a retrospection of his own career, of
the many errors committed, of the wrong bias
of his life—all sources of discouragement and
irritation concealed under an appearance of
nonchalant cheerfulness. Yes, the clearer his
perception of his blunders and weaknesses, the
closer did he conceal his regrets. Though his
love of virtue prevented self-forgiveness, it was
not strong enough to make him alter his course
—no, he dared not risk taking on himself the
responsibilities of a family.

It was after having so decided that he returned to Château Ste. Marie. In the meantime, Pauline and little Alix d'Allot had been
to vespers, remaining during the children's
catechism, and then Madame Rendu ordered
the carriage, resolutely refusing to remain to
supper. She had no desire to meet Vilpont
again. She had always disliked him—now
she had begun to fear him.

During the drive home she delivered an
oration against Paris and Parisians. Little
Mademoiselle d'Allot, whom the vexed woman
had forgotten, fired up at this abuse of her
native city, and said bravely, " All Provincials
hate the capital—I'm sure *we* don't care."

Had Madame Rendu been as crafty as she was honest, she would have refrained from that diatribe—she would have taken into account that spirit of contradiction which exists in the best of human beings, and the sympathy excited in generous dispositions by anything bordering on injustice. Too much praise often renders hearers antagonistic; too much abuse as often turns them into partisans. In this instance Pauline's heart burned within her. For the first time in her life she thought her mother wrong. And thus it came to pass that mother's apprehensions and maiden's awakening preference jarred painfully. The hero had appeared, and had cast his glamour over the inexperienced heroine.

Pauline did not frolic as usual round her father when she bade him good-night, and tendered her brow to her mother in silence. As soon as she was in her own room, she let fall her hair—such wonderful hair!—as though it were an offence to her; but this vexed mood did not last long. Pauline's disposition was too sweet for that, and her good angel was about to whisper to her.

In a recess was a small oratory—one of the delights of Pauline's life. Her father, whose single sentiment was admiration of his daughter, had procured for her a Madonna, one of Clesinger's marble wonders—a real gem of art —and winter and summer Pauline found means to surround this loved image with fresh flowers. As she knelt down to say her evening prayers, tears, repentant tears, rolled over her cheeks. No words could have been so eloquent as the silent, unspoken petition for grace to overcome self-will, for help to be obedient, for pardon for the rebellious anger she had felt.

She rose from her knees full of heroic resolution, the first-fruit of which was, that she put her ivory-bound mass-book into a drawer with a studiously careless touch.

# CHAPTER XI.

## THE CONSEQUENCES OF NOT DOING AS OTHERS DO.

PAULINE was as merry as a cricket on the Monday. In the early morning she practised her scale; afterwards attended madame on her round to the kitchen, putting her little nose into every culinary preparation, as though she cared immensely about it. That duty performed, she dressed madame's hair, and then her own, making her head a marvel of intricacy and neatness.

Madame Rendu watched her closely through the day, and came at last to the conclusion that she had frightened herself about nothing, and that the child was fancy free. It had been like a stab to her heart even to surmise that a daughter of hers, educated on the system approved by generation after generation, should lapse into the novelty of preferring one man to another, until authorized by her parents to do so. Relieved from the awful dread of town-talk—that irreparable misfortune when a young girl is the cause of it—Madame Rendu was able to receive all her friends with her usual indifference, bordering on hostility. She could even join in the laugh at Madame Jorey's *tête-à-tête* with such a man as Vilpont, though she refused to go so far as Gonde, who had set about the report that the young man was trying to cajole the old lady into matrimony. It was Gonde who first called him madame's bijou.

For the present, at least, this stupid gossip did not reach Ste. Marie. Pauline heard everything that was said or supposed on the subject, and kept a proper maidenly silence, It is astonishing how well girls *can* hide their feelings. Her one dread was lest it should be suspected how these discussions pained her. She had been ignorant of even what dislike was; now she positively hated all these busy-bodies and slanderers.

How dared they think and speak disrespect-fully of her godmother, so venerable and good a woman! This dear little dove often shook with anger, but with some of the wisdom of the serpent, held her peace. It is to be hoped that when she went to confession, she accused herself honestly of the anger and hatred swell-ing her breast.

It was a time-honored custom that the Ren-dus should go to Ste. Marie for the first day of the vintage. Pauline had been taken there a baby in arms—had gathered grapes there as child and school-girl. The least alteration in a custom so well known, and Madame Rendu knew what would be the consequence. There would be whispers, and conjectures breeding lies. One day, only one day more, could not signify much, even though Vilpont were Satan in person; and then she would take to her bed rather than put her foot into Ste. Marie again until it was clear of so embarrassing an inmate. The same instinct which makes the barn-door fowl stretch her wings over her brood while the hawk is yet but a distant black speck in the sky, was agitating Madame Rendu's maternal breast.

Pauline said many more prayers than usual, and tried hard not to be happier at the thought of this first day of the vintage than she had ever been before. She imposed secret penances on herself, said a hundred *Aves* and *Paters* a day, and fasted so bravely that her mother had to scold her into taking something more than bread and *bouillon*. The happiness, however, refused to be starved, and was in full strength when the day arrived.

Was all this merry jingle of joy-bells in her heart because she should see one thin, dark face once more? Just so. She had not yet passed beyond that stage when the mere presence of one particular person is happiness. Her conscience pricked her for this gladness; for she knew full well her mother's hostile feelings, and it was conscience made this dear heart put on her least fresh and becoming dress.

"You cannot go that figure!" exclaimed Madame Rendu. "What is the meaning of your putting on that shabby frock?"

"I thought you would like it best," said Pauline coloring, and looking down.

"Of a piece with your fasting," said the

mother severely. "You have been doing all
you can to worry me this week past."

"O mamma! if you only knew, it was for
█best—indeed it was!"

"You should let your mother guide you,
and not be trying to guide yourself. Go now
and put on your new *barège*, and be quick."

Mademoiselle was well pleased when she
saw herself in her pretty fresh costume; she
looked, for all the world, like a shepherdess
by Boucher, and it is certain she did not give
one regret to her lost good intention.

"No wandering from the others," was
Madame Rendu's warning as they stopped at
the gates of the Château.

"How late you are!" shouted Madame
Jorey from a back door; "they are all gone
this hour past. Run, Pauline, you'll find them
in Vigne des Trois Frères. Stop, give me a
kiss first," and the old lady gave her one of
those hugs that deep-chested old ladies alone
can give—a kiss like the snap of a pistol, the
kiss of a practical godmother, who did not
understand silent pressure of lips.

"Send one of the girls with her," said Madame Rendu; "she cannot go alone." A
*Manon* or *Manette* was caught, and with this
chaperone required by French custom Pauline
set off, soberly as long as she was in sight of
the elders, but like an arrow from the bow
when they had turned the corner. The vineyard
was noisy with shouts and song and laughter,

the valley with the sound of hammers on the empty sides of barrels.

A dozen young ladies of the higher and lower and lowest *bourgeoisie* were already picking, eating, talking, singing. Some of the papas were there as guards, and some worthy matrons of no *bourgeoisie* at all; some of the girls' brothers, boys from twelve to fifteen, were of the party, and M. Vilpont, apparently one of the most industrious gatherers.

The moment Pauline caught sight of him she turned in the opposite direction. She joined a group of Ste. Marie girls, and talked and joked and laughed as much as any of the most thoughtless. This answered very well for a time, but presently she often forgot to reply or to laugh. Her prayers had been heard, but her joyful feelings were fast fading away. A tender word spoken at that instant would have made her cry fit to break her heart, and she could not have explained to herself why. She grew tired of girls and grapes, and wandered away; she wanted to be alone.

Vilpont, on his side, was conscientiously acting up to his last resolve—for Pauline's dear sake he would avoid Pauline.

And so Pauline went further and further from the grape-gatherers, her small figure easily lost to sight among the thick bushes. She had no plan, no object in view, save like all hurt creatures to get away and hide.

St. Gloi lies in a punch-bowl shaped valley, the low hills round it rising gradually until, as they reach Ste. Marie, they attain a considerable height. These hills, as has been before described, are cut by deep ravines or gorges, the beds of mountain-streams, feeders of the lake. Mere rivulets in fine weather, during the *trombes* so frequent in the district these streams become swift torrents, dangerous to cross. These *trombes* come on with great suddenness and with a fury beyond imagination. First a far-spreading cloud darkens the sky, and a moment after hill and plain are hidden by thick, slanting rain, a wall of water that seems to reach from earth to heaven, hiding both.

The morning had been sultry, without sun and breezeless. As the day advanced, all blue vanished from the sky. About noon the warning darkness showed itself; a moment later there was a loud cry—"The *trombe!* the *trombe* is coming!" and every one set off full speed down paths along which they would in cool blood have picked their way cautiously. Then the heavens opened, and the rain fell; yet not like rain—it hit with the force of pebbles, accompanied by a muffled roar more terrifying than the loudest claps of thunder. It terrified the more, that no one knew its cause. *Échalas* mingled with vine-branches whirled through the air, while the very ground seemed slipping from beneath the feet. The road at the bottom of the hill had now become a rushing river, across which the men carried the young girls, getting the women over by placing one between two men. The greater number rushed into the large outhouses of the Château, while those who dared crowded into kitchen and parlor. At first the confusion and hubbub were so great that there was no knowing who was or was not there. Madame Rendu's voice at last made itself heard—

"Pauline, where are you?" No reply. "Good God!" she screamed, "where's Pauline?"

A great silence fell on all present. Vilpont made one spring out of the room, the mother's screams rending his ears. He knew that other men were on his steps, but he asked neither counsel nor companionship. He had seen, without seeming to do so, the girl leave her companions, and he had guessed something of why she did so; and now remorse filled his heart, as though he was to blame for whatever might happen to her. Buffeting against the storm, repeatedly beaten back or thrown down, he thought with horror of how impossible for that slight child to withstand what rendered him, a man in his full vigor, sometimes helpless. Where was he to seek her? He had no clue save that she had gone to the left of where they had been gathering grapes. But where was that vineyard? He could scarcely see two feet before him for the blinding rain. He staggered up the side of the hill nearest the house to seek for steps or pathway, often obliged to lie down to escape some whirling échalas. The wind was still tearing off leaves, scattering grapes; but the actual vine itself

held its own where there was no landslip. He
shouted out from time to time Pauline's name.
He knew it was a vain effort against the roar
of wind and the swish of rain, but he could not
resist doing so.

Luckily, no storm but has its period of ex-
haustion, and presently there was a lull; the
rain was less heavy, less serried. He was able
to see the chimneys of the Château. This
cheered him, in spite of its showing how little
way he had made, for it made him sure he had
not missed the course he wished to take.

Happy to think that others were seeking in
other directions, in case he should be on the
wrong tack, he toiled on until he came to the
edge of the very gorge where, the evening before, he had sat and pondered as to his own
life. Instead of the gurgling of the rivulet
that had made its quiet song the accompaniment of his meditation, he now heard the
rush of a torrent. If she had really come
this way, she might have taken shelter among
the brushwood, or she might have crossed to
the other side before the storm burst, and have
been unable to return. He made a trumpet
of his hands, and shouted " Pauline !" Surely
there was a reply—a faint yet shrill sound.
Griping his mother earth with feet and hands,
he let himself down the bank. No easy task,
for a false step might precipitate him into the
angry water below.

Once down, he again shouted "Pauline !"
This time he was clearly answered, but not

for the life of him could he tell from whence. Holding by the scrubby wood, he went a few yards up, then a few yards the other way, then he sprang up as if a shot had been fired at his ear when a well-known voice said :

" I am here, monsieur."

" Where ? " he asked, staring about, and then a little figure came almost on its knees from under a bush.

He caught her in his arms, and she nestled her head on his bosom softly, crying, and he keeping her company.

It would have made all the hair of all the heads in St. Gloi bristle like porcupine-quills had they witnessed the scene. Propriety and prudence were just then absent. Of course this did not last long ; violent emotions have their lulls as well as other storms.

Pauline once more stood on her feet, but shivering, and holding fast Vilpont's arm.

" I have been so frightened," she said, apologetically.

" Not so frightened as I have been," he replied ; " but that's over for us. We must make haste back, for your father and mother's sake."

" Oh yes, monsieur. Let us go as fast as possible."

" Do you know any way except through the vines, mademoiselle ? "

Propriety had returned.

" There are some steps leading to the road, close to the top of this bank," she replied.

"Very good; but first we must get up the bank, and I am afraid you must hold on by the tails of my coat. I see no other way by which I can help you, for I must myself grapple the bushes with both hands. There, do not let go."

She obeyed him quietly, and they got to the top without an accident.

"Now you must be the guide. Thank God, it only rains." But how it did rain. There was no possibility of walking arm in arm; they had to go single file.

Suddenly they heard the church-bells begin to ring.

"That must be for us," said Pauline, and Vilpont heard her whispering a prayer.

Straight forward they went; but when they reached where the steps ought to have been, they found instead a high barrier of earth. There had been a landslip from above.

"It was so much the shortest way," sighed Pauline.

"There's a monster of a cloud rising, mademoiselle," said Vilpont. "We must get over, and lose no time, either."

"Very well, monsieur."

He crawled over one heap of stones and then another, pulling her after him. There was not much light, but sufficient for him to perceive that she had nothing but stockings on her feet.

"Great Heaven!" he said, "where have you lost your boots?"

"I was on the other side of the gully when the storm began, and I took them off to cross over; and the water rushed so, I let them drop." Here her bravery broke down, and tears ran over her face—tears of pain; her feet were cut and bruised, and but for the mud, he would have seen they were bleeding.

As soon as they had crossed over the barrier, he said, "You must allow me to carry you; luckily you are just the weight I am up to."

"I can walk, indeed I can. Oh, pray let me!" as he put his arm round her. "Mamma would never forgive me. Oh, pray, pray! I don't mind the pain."

There was such a beseeching terror in her voice and face that he gave up the point. "Take my arm, at least," and she felt him wince every time she did so. When once she could not repress a faint cry, he said, "Do let me." But she shook her head, saying, "It's for mamma's sake I refuse."

"Sit down then, and let me wrap my handkerchief round your feet."

She was so weary and sore that she let him have his way. He tore his cravat and handkerchief into bands, and kneeling before her; bound up the poor torn feet. She saw how his face was working, and laying her hand softly on his shoulder, she said:

"Do not be so sorry for me; it seems worse than it is. And indeed I would let you carry me, but it would vex mamma. People are so severe."

5*

"Le diable les emporte," he said savagely, because he was so much grieved.

At last they were in the road; and just as always happens in similar cases, no sooner was there no need of help, plenty was at hand.

First came the Curé. As soon as she saw him, Pauline let go Vilpont's arm, and clung to that of her old friend.

"Where's papa?" were her first words.

"On the opposite side, my poor little one; but we shall soon have him back."

"Monsieur found me," said Pauline.

"Très-bien, très-bien," was M. le Curé's reply; but he would rather she had been rescued by one of the *vignerons* now joining them.

They raised a loud shout to give notice that the missing lamb was found, and then set off in chase of M. Rendu and those with him.

At first Madame Rendu behaved as mothers usually do when they receive back a child who has been in peril—she kissed and hugged her, and cried and scolded. But when she heard who had rescued Pauline, her annoyance banished all other feeling.

"That man is always in the way," she said.

Vilpont luckily was not present, and Pauline made no defence; she was thinking how best to hide the way her feet had been bandaged. She knew too well her country's rigorous notions about young ladies, not to dread her mother's discovering what she had allowed Vilpont to do. She was indeed so anxious to escape any questionings, that she submitted in silence to all Madame Rendu's commands.

"You must go to bed, child, as soon as your feet have been bathed—that's the only fit place for you. Why couldn't you stay with the rest? Don't you see, Pauline, that it is not doing as others do that gets you into trouble."

# CHAPTER XII.

## MADAME RENDU TO THE RESCUE.

HAVING safely ensconced Pauline in a warm bed, Madame Rendu went down to the *salon* with some composure. She had quite decided on her course of conduct with regard to Vilpont.

Here it may be as well to remark that different countries have different habits and different notions on almost all points. The proverb says, " Do at Rome as the Romans do," which plainly means that the Romans have peculiar ways of their own ; so have the Turks, so have the English, and so have the French. Now, one well-established custom among our nearest neighbors is a strictness with regard to girls unknown in this country. There are small opportunities allowed for flirtation ; and such an adventure as Pauline's might be a serious disadvantage to her, of which her mother was perfectly aware. Englishwomen are shocked, and no wonder, at what is implied by such a surveillance, and by anxiety like that of Madame Rendu ; but she, on her side, would have been horrified by the independent ways on this side of the Channel. The difference lies in a nutshell : an English girl is taught that she can and ought to take care of herself,

and a French one that she is to be taken care
of. Madame Rendu is neither to be wondered
at nor blamed for what she felt, or for what she
said to Vilpont.

"Monsieur, if you are a man of honor, you
will allow no one to know of your being the
one who found my child. It would have been
better had you refrained from interference in
what did not concern you."

Vilpont understood and pardoned her bitter-
ness. He replied, "From me, madame, you
have nothing to fear; but the fact is already
known to half a dozen people who met us."

She turned away, her heart burning with re-
sentment against this man. It was lucky for
her reason that she never would know certain
facts attending the rescue.

Once satisfied that Pauline was found, and
safe in her mother's care, Madame Jorey was
too much taken up with providing for the
wants of all the people crowded into her
kitchen to have leisure for curiosity. But she
found a moment luckily to go and see her god-
daughter before joining her visitors in the
*salon.*

"You little coward! what are you crying
about now?" she began, as the little white,
tearful face was turned up to her gaze.

"*Chère marraine,* mamma is so vexed about
my being lost, and—that—M. Vilpont was the
one to find me. I knew she would be; but it
was not my fault, and it was very good of him
to take so much trouble about me. Only,

mamma is angry; and oh! please don't talk about it downstairs."

Madame Jorey did not look much pleased either.

"What made you run away from the others?" she asked.

A silence.

"I hope you are not crying about anything save your mother's anger. There; don't look so frightened. I am not going to ask you any more questions. What's done is done. It's a lesson, god-daughter."

Madame Jorey, thus forewarned, showed such an entire want of curiosity as was thoroughly unnatural. But all those in the *salon* were equally willing with herself to let the matter pass in silence. *Bonne maman* was besides preoccupied by household cares. Rooms must be prepared for M. and Mme. Rendu, the weather being again so wild that their return to St. Gloi was impossible, even had it been wise to remove Pauline.

During one of his hostess's flights upstairs, Vilpont stopped her, saying that he should be glad of half an hour's conversation with her.

"Come away at once," she said. "To tell the truth, Madame Rendu is not the pleasantest of company just now. Let me see, where can I take you so as to be out of the way of all these people? The *office* (the store-room) will be the safest."

There, amid the combined odors of candles, sugar, oil, coffee, preserves, onions, jellies,

hams, soap, lemons, and spices, did Vilpont
confide to her something that made the good
lady both wink and stare. She accompanied
his narration by many of those interjectional
exclamations we should call swearing in this
country. When he ended, she said—

"This is not one of your romances that you
have been telling me?"

"All true as the most commonplace reality."

"And you are in earnest?"

"Perfectly."

"Well—well—well! Sleep on it, and if you
remain in the same mind after twenty-four
hours, tell me so, and I will see what I can do.
I cannot take it all in so quickly. I must turn
it over in my own mind. I am well-nigh
crazed with that wind—more than half the
wine-crop lost."

The following morning was quiet and gray,
an air of languor pervaded people and country
—a sort of physical weariness. Madame Jorey
was, however, an exception. As brisk as
usual, she was sallying forth to see the damage
done to her vines when she met Vilpont.

"Not yet," she said. "Your business can
wait, mine cannot. I said twenty-four hours,
and that will bring us to seven in the evening."

Some of the people loitering about remarked that the madame and her guest spoke
in whispers and with gravity.

"A marriage," said the women.

"At her age?" laughed the men.

"There are younger in the house," was the rejoinder of a sharp-sighted girl.

None of us can walk invisible, or find a covering thick enough under which to hide our secrets.

As they were returning (for Vilpont had accompanied Madame Jorey on her tour of inspection), they met the Rendus' *calèche*, in which were father, mother, and Pauline.

"But how, and why, and wherefore?" screamed Madame Jorey.

"We are taking Pauline home to see her own doctor," explained Madame Rendu, her black eyes stabbing all round. M. Rendu looked heavy, as a man does who has passed a sleepless night.

Pauline's eyes were downcast, but she flushed and paled rapidly.

"À l'avantage!" said Madame Rendu ceremoniously. "Allons, Pierre," to the coachman.

"Allons, Pierre—en route," repeated M. Rendu, and the carriage drove on

"What a woman!" said Madame Jorey laughing.

Vilpont pulled at his moustaches.

"But she is right," went on *bonne maman;* "she is doing her duty as a mother."

# CHAPTER XIII.

## JACTA ALEA EST.

" My story ! " said Vilpont at the end of the twenty-four hours Madame Jorey had stipulated he should take for reflection,—" a few words will suffice.

" My father was the Vicomte de Kergeac, the younger brother of the present marquis of that name, of a family more Royalist than the king himself, Henri V. *bien entendu*. My uncle is the most furious Legitimist of the present day,—the most narrow-minded and honestest man I ever knew.

" As a matter of course my father left the army after 1830—was one of those who saw Charles X. safe out of France—who conspired with Madame du Berri ; and being fortunate enough to escape any other exile than that of his brother's château, married a girl beautiful, good, and poor in proportion. He died shortly after my birth of the effect of his wounds, leaving his wife and two boys, of whom I was the younger, to the care of the marquis.

" I received little notice from my uncle ; all his interest centred in my brother, heir to his title and poverty. The marquis himself, I ought to have told you, was a childless widower. It was to Adhemar he expounded our family history, and whom he initiated in the intricacies of our heraldic devices—a study I have never mastered.

"I was my mother's companion; and seeing me what I am, you will wonder to hear that I was looked upon then as a little saint. I was nourished on lives of saints, on hymns, on legends of miracles. From the time I could walk alone, I took my part in holy processions and *Pardons*, of which Bretagne is the country *par excellence*. One of my greatest delights was to officiate as the curé's assistant at mass—my usual reward for good conduct during the week.

"Whether from this apparent vocation, or from family tradition, which made the Church provide for younger sons, I cannot say, but the fact is, I was destined for the priesthood."

Here Madame Jorey exclaimed, "Tiens, tiens!" lifting up her arms, her amazement not unmingled with a sort of comic horror.

"At twelve years of age," went on Vilpont, "I was sent to the Petit Seminaire, and at fifteen was on the point of being transferred to the Grand Seminaire, when my brother died from the effects of a fall from his horse.

"The fathers parted from me with regret. They considered me a promising pupil, one that might became powerful as an eloquent preacher."

Madame Jorey shook her head.

"Who can say that I might not have been another Bossuet?" continued Vilpont. Sermons and comedies have much the same end in view—to point out and condemn the errors and vices of the day. However, the *soutane* could not be allowed to extinguish the name of De Kergeac.

"As long as my mother lived I remained at the château. I should never have left her, had she survived till I was gray-headed. But she left me."—Here came a pause.—"I cannot talk of her; her image, till quite lately, has laid like a seal upon my heart, shutting out any other inmate.

"It was after that the struggle began between the marquis and me—astonishing how insufferable excellent people can be. Prejudice has a chemistry of its own, by which it transforms our best impulses into bad ones. At the best, constant contact has in it something irritating. Even kindness itself will sometimes exasperate. What then must be the result of forced companionship between two persons with peculiarities that gave out sparks the moment they met? The marquis belonged to the old world, and I to the new. He had taken it for granted I should prove another Adhemar, and bury myself willingly in the old château, with its parchments, traditions, and hopes of the return of Henry V. Perhaps the strength of a sentiment is in proportion to its being a single one. In the marquis's case it isolated him from all other perceptions.

"As I told you before, we separated. I made him the sacrifice of not entering any profession which could possibly bring me in contact with the Government. He had been a careful guardian, and he put me at once in possession of my father and mother's small fortune, with the accumulated interest since my father's death. I went to Paris, dropped my title, and you know the rest."

"Well!" exclaimed Madame Jorey, and there was a whole series of interrogations in that exclamation.

He answered, "I was, and I am perfectly serious in begging you to make my proposal for Mademoiselle Pauline known to M. and Mme. Rendu. If I do not marry Mademoiselle Rendu, I shall never have a wife."

"The wind carrieth away words and feathers," observed the old lady. "It's my belief you are only half-minded in this proposal. Take my advice: go away to your painted faces."

"Impossible, till I have an answer."

"You must give me all your credentials," she began. "The title and address of your uncle, the marquis, that of your medical man and your confessor."

He wrote on one of his own cards.

"There is the title and address of my uncle. As for the others, I have neither doctor for body or soul."

Madame Jorey did not actually whistle, but she screwed up her lips as if she were about to do so.

"No profession, or worse than none—no re-

ligion—a downright Bohemian! Don't pro-
pose, M. Vilpont; you will be refused.
Though I like you, it's in spite of myself, and
I could not advise your being accepted."

"You would refuse me for one of your
grand-daughters?"

"As flat as a pancake, my dear friend. You
are not one of us, neither by birth, nor education, nor habits. What we hold sacred is a
matter of indifference to you. Our ways look
mean to you. We call you a free-thinker, and
you call us bigots. I look on you as one of
the best specimens of the butterfly race, but
that is all. There, take it in good part; go
your way, and leave us to go ours."

"You will not force me to beg Madame
Chamband's assistance?"

It was a capital move, and checkmated the
good lady.

"No, no; let us keep clear of that chattering
pie."

When Vilpont had seen Madame Jorey set
off for St. Gloi, how did he feel? Muttering
to himself, "Jacta alea est," he set off on one
of his long walks. "Fate," so ran his thoughts
—"fate is too strong for the strongest among
us. The death of an old '93 man brings about
an unforeseen visit, a thunderstorm, and a
frightened girl, and my life undergoes, probably, an utter change. Has man any free-will?
Are we not constantly compelled to do what,
if our will were free, we would not do. Circumstances weave the web of all our lives, not

our own determination." Destiny rose up before him grave and sad.

No thinking man about to link another life with his own, but must look forward with as much anxiety as hope. Vilpont could not obliterate his experiences of life; echoes of the past were in his ears. He had known so many set out gayly on the route he was proposing to traverse, who had been forced to cover their heads with ashes, and to bow down before grief and shame.

There was one fatality, however, of which he forgot to think—that which is made by ourselves, by our errors, or by defects which cause our errors. Faults and evil experiences were demanding a penalty from him at this moment. He could not silence some questions. With the admiration and tenderness he undoubtedly felt for Pauline there was strangely mingled a sense of disparity—her innocence and purity with the lees of a lawless life.

Love (he had written it over and over again) was the meeting of two beings in perfect accord. And between this gracious child and himself was this possible? He told himself bitterly enough that though angels rejoice over the repentant sinner, there is no account of how the sinner feels in company with the angels. He had a wretched suspicion that even loved by and loving Pauline he might weary of his existence. Had he not a horror of a long-continued course of fine weather? Had he not tired of blue skies and gentle zephyrs?

Was constancy possible for him? Was he not always curious about the unknown?

And how should he dare to write as he had done with a madame at his fireside. His talent (and consequently his independence) was bound up and limited by his pictures of the realities of the day.

And yet his whole soul revolted when he thought of the great probability that Madame Rendu would refuse him. And he expected she would do so; for he knew there was nothing so unconquerable as one of those dislikes without any reasonable foundation, and he felt that dislike was a mild term to apply to Madame Rendu's feelings towards him.

And now, how about the little heroine of all these meditations and consultations?

# CHAPTER XIV.

### BONNE MAMAN ADVERSARY AND PARTISAN.

"I WILL have no gossiping about yesterday," said Madame Rendu, as they sat down to the eleven o'clock breakfast. "By this time it will be known to all our neighbors that we remained the night at Château Ste. Marie; every one will be calling to know why. Let them hear you practising, for I don't choose that you should have to explain about your feet. To-morrow, whatever it makes you suffer, you must go out."

"But Pierre knows, mamma; and if we don't tell ourselves, some wrong story will get wind."

"Do you think in your wisdom that the truth is ever believed? However, I will not allow you to dispute with me; you will have to give up your love of contradiction, Pauline, if you ever mean to be happy. Go and do as I bid you; as long as you are single, I shall take care you are not one of the young ladies who are talked about."

Madame Rendu was equal to the occasion; she entered at once on the subject of the storm, described her own terrors, and her thankfulness when she saw Pauline return leaning on the arm of the Curé. Some rumors were already floating about as to Pau-

line's having been lost. Madame Rendu
laughed, saying how ingeniously some people
worked up truth and fiction. How could she
be lost in the vineyard close to the Château,
in a place she knew as well as she did the
street she lived in. This arrangement of the
subject, coupled with the sound of Pauline's
piano, hid the truth for the time being. Madame Rendu resorted to another device to
keep it concealed in the future.

She mentioned to Madame Chambaud, in
the strictest confidence, that she was about to
give a ball to celebrate Pauline's twentieth
birthday. Did Madame Chambaud think that
a fancy-ball would be ill-judged? "But it
would be charming, charming!" vouched Madame Chambaud. Of course this secret was
known all over St. Gloi before night, as
Madame Rendu had confidently expected ; and
as one nail drives out another, so did this report drive away all others.

Successful in all that regarded the outside
of the affair, Madame Rendu could only
smother, not eradicate, her secret anxieties.
Some instinct made her refrain from question-
ing Pauline as to Vilpont's finding her. She
dreaded the knowledge she might acquire ;
for she knew if Pauline spoke, she would tell
the truth, and all the truth. And what if this
truth shackled her with any obligations to this
writer of plays, this man without a position.

Pauline presented to her mother's view an
unruffled surface. "Ah!" thought the ma-

tron, "give me anything in the world to find out but a girl's feelings." And she was right; space, matter, numbers, may come to be explained; but how make clear a problem that a young girl will not herself seek to solve? It is a point of honor with a respectable French mother to give her daughter to a husband with a heart like a blank sheet of paper; and Madame Rendu really suffered in suspecting that this could never now be the case with Pauline.

A thought of the man she thus dreaded offering to become her son-in-law was as far from her mind as that the Sultan or the Prince of Wales would do so. Yet the moment she saw Madame Jorey get out of her cabriolet dressed in her best gown, she guessed the purport of her visit, and at once called M. Rendu, not to ask his opinion, but to hear her decision.

Madame Jorey certainly disapproved of Vilpont as a husband for Pauline, but is it difficult to accept a mission of confidence and to keep clear of partisanship? It was long since *bonne maman's* heart had beat so fast as when she met the glance of Madame Rendu's hard eyes. The lengthy interchange of compliments and inquiries gave the ambassadress time to recover her usual *sang froid*.

"How is Pauline?" she began.

"Very well; she only required a day's rest. She got up as well as ever this morning, and is at the *ouvroir*." *

* *Ouvroir*, work-room superintended by charitable ladies.

M. Rendu now appeared, and there was a renewal of compliments and salutations. Then Madame Jorey, yielding to necessity, opened her communication.

"I bring a proposal of marriage for my goddaughter from a future marquis, an old Breton noble."

Madame Rendu was startled for an instant by the unexpected announcement.

"His name?" she asked.

"M. Alberic Vilpont, Vicomte de Kergeac," said Madame Jorey, pompously and solemnly.

"You need not go on, my dear lady," said Madame Rendu promptly, and stretching out her feet, a gesture of contempt well known to all her acquaintance. "We refuse absolutely," she added, accentuating each word.

"My wife, my wife," interposed M. Rendu, "let us at least hear what our excellent friend has to say."

"What can she say, but that this man is without religion or morals? He has never put his foot into a church since he has been here."

"Pardon me," interrupted Madame Jorey; "he went with us."

"Yes, true, with the girls, as he would have gone to a play. But leaving that point, I have sufficient reasons for my decision: first, his immoral writings; and secondly, his vagabond ways. Why does he go about under false pretences? why conceal his name and rank?"

"Easy to explain;" and Madame Jorey related what Vilpont had told her of his story.

Madame Rendu listened as we do when we have made up our mind beforehand, and are decided to let no argument influence us.

"I regret this proposal," she said when Madame Jorey concluded, "and I am sure M. Rendu agrees with me. Were M. Vilpont ten times as noble, ten times as famous, ten times as rich, I would say the same. I look on him as an example of all that is worst in our country. I would as soon sign Pauline's death-warrant as her marriage contract with him."

A deep sigh made them all turn round: Pauline was standing at the inner door of communication.

"Mademoiselle," said her mother, "retire to your own room."

Pauline vanished almost before the order was pronounced. She had not even a thought of claiming a voice in the decision of her fate.

As M. Rendu led Madame Jorey downstairs to put her into her cabriolet, he said in a low voice, "I beg you will thank M. Vilpont for the honor he has done us; but you see, we think it is best for us *bourgeois* to keep to our own class; we could not bear to be separated from our child."

"As for what I tell the Vicomte de Kergeac, I shall use my own discretion, *père* Rendu. I confess I don't think Madame Rendu wrong, though she might have been more polite. I am sorry for the lad, I like him; and when I like, I like; and when I hate, it's with all my heart."

Madame Jorey did use her own discretion, which led her to be more candid than compassionate in the account she gave Vilpont of the interview with the Rendus. She entirely omitted to mention Pauline's sigh or how pale and pitiful her face.

Vilpont changed color so violently that the old lady paused and repented. She then bustled away, returning presently with a glass of wine, "Drink that," she said; "I have not given a drop of it to a soul since Jorey died."

He put aside the wine with a "Thank you, I do not need that kind of support." After a short silence he went on, "I sincerely intended to try and make Mademoiselle Pauline happy, and with her sweet disposition the task would not have been a hard one. That is now a past hope. Perhaps you will not think it wrong to tell her how entirely I admired and reverenced her."

"Better let that alone," replied *bonne maman*, "girls' hearts are such tender things. When I was seventeen, my dear sir, I was ready to marry any man, and to believe I loved him. Don't fancy I am not your friend because I say I think Madame Rendu has done wisely. How can a girl judge a man as well as a mother?"

"Discussion on that point now is useless; I would rather thank you for all your goodness to me. I shall never forget Ste. Marie les Vignes and its kind *châtelaine*." Vilpont took her hand and kissed it. *Bonne maman*

reddened prodigiously, then went away as fast
as she could, making a portentous noise with
her handkerchief. Vilpont busied himself at
once with preparations for leaving the following day. He did not see his hostess again till
dinner; she kept out of his way, actually
dreading to meet him. To her surprise, he
met her with his usual composure, and exert-
ing all his powers of pleasing, so won on the
poor lady, that she came over quite to his side.
In spite of his efforts, or rather in consequence
of them, she grew more and more fidgety and
low-spirited, and this state of her mind will
excuse the useless thing she afterwards did.
A letter from Pauline was given to her just as
Vilpont had gone out to smoke his cigar.

Pauline had written but a few lines—

" DEAR MARRAINE,—I have a favor to beg,
now that it is all over. It will make me happier if you will ask M. Vilpont to forgive me for
once being rude to him, very rude. I said one
evening, meaning him to hear me, that I had
gone to sleep while his beautiful poem was
being read. It was not true. I had heard
every word. I was ashamed at having cried.
I wanted to vex him ; just my bad temper, I
could not help it. I should not like him to go
away thinking ill of me, dear *marraine*.
Please to tell him.—Your respectful, loving
godchild,                              PAULINE."

Madame Jorey put this poor effusion into
Vilpont's hand.

He read it through. "Tell her," he began, and suddenly broke down. He covered his face; his chest heaved as when a man weeps; *bonne maman* was first struck speechless and motionless, then she rushed at him, stroking his hair as if he had been a little child, muttering the inevitable, "Tiens, tiens, tiens!"

# CHAPTER XV.

## FRENCH CUSTOM SINCE ADAM DELVED.

*"Can a bird fall in a snare upon the earth where no gin
is set for him."*

DURING the following two years Stephanie
Jorey was married to M. de Saye, and her sister Julie became the wife of a rich Lyons
manufacturer. " Unexceptionable marriages
—charming households —*jolis ménages!*"
chorused the Joreys and their relations.

M. de Saye had first proposed for Pauline ;
but Pauline on that occasion found sufficient
courage to express an unconditional refusal.

" I must at least not loathe my husband,"
she said, with a flash of anger, and Madame
Rendu was silenced.

This occurred while Pauline's recollection
of the day in the vineyard was in all its freshness. She had, besides, a foolish idea that it
was treachery in M. de Saye to wish to sup-
plant his friend.

Poor Madame Rendu, notwithstanding her
strong will, her prudence, and her fancy-ball,
had not succeeded in keeping out of the do-
main of gossip what Madame Chambaud called " The Vilpont Romance."

Alfred de Musset says somewhere that
" everything is known save that which is un-

known." So it proved in this case. Within forty-eight hours after old Madame Jorey's official visit to the Rendus, Vilpont's rescue of the lost damsel, his offer of marriage, his title and expectations, were discussed by every man and woman in St. Gloi. What they never knew was what had passed during the *tête-à-tête* walk, when those few words had been spoken, awakening new feelings in Pauline; words on which hinged all the future happiness or unhappiness of her life.

Madame Rendu had been forced to give up her Sisyphean task of stemming questions— the tyranny of intimacy had forced her to speak out; that is, she had given facts, as bare as it was possible.

A stern follower of the social code of her country, that *her* daughter should have been compelled by untoward fate to infringe one of its strictest articles, fretted her spirit to a point of exasperation that English mothers will scarcely understand. The Frenchwoman knew she had to reckon with the traditional prejudices and customs of her nation, all dead against a *tête-à-tête* between a girl and any man not her father or brother.

"Very well for you English," says the Frenchman; but "*mon cher*, such freedom does not answer with us."

Judge Madame Rendu, therefore, by French, and not British social laws.

For perhaps the first time in her life, Pauline's mother had a doubt of her own wis-

6*

dom. She was assailed by a secret fear that Pauline's "heart had spoken" before leave given—another grave infraction of rules—and this fear made her doubt whether she had done wisely in giving Vilpont so summary a dismissal. Impossible to deny that he had acted delicately and honorably; it was infinitely painful to her to doubt her own judgment, but she had strength of will enough never to breathe to human being that she had been in any uncertainty as to her own infallibility. She continued to abstain from all investigations of Pauline's feelings, being aware of the gulf which divides conjecture from knowledge.

The first left her unhampered; the last would have prevented her urging Pauline to accept M. de Saye.

On whatever indications might be founded Madame Rendu's misgivings, none of those who saw Pauline intimately ever came near a supposition that the girl nourished any regrets. She took the liveliest interest in the trousseaux of her two friends, accepted cheerfully the office of *demoiselle d'honneur* on the occasion of their marriages, and was so amiable and friendly to M. de Saye, that he more than once wondered if the refusal of his offer had not come from the mother alone.

Vilpont, in De Saye's place, would never have doubted at all. The amiability and friendliness of young ladies towards gentlemen bears many interpretations.

During the summer of that year the Rendus went to Switzerland, extending their journey to the Italian lakes. Such a departure from their custom of going to the baths of S—— naturally excited comment. Like all small towns which are isolated, as it were, from general interests, St. Gloi fell back on the private affairs of its citizens—nothing, as we know, too trivial to be talked about.

" There is no understanding the Rendu politics," observed Madame Chambaud—" travelling when they ought to be marrying their daughter. Pauline is twenty-two, and she is just the sort of girl to lose her looks early. Only classical features can bear the want of the freshness of youth."

" You forget how accomplished she is," replied Madame Edmond Jorcy, the words meaning one thing, the intonation another.

" After all, dear madame, there is compensation for everything. Stephanie and Julie, who claim no superiority, are happy wives and mothers. Poor Pauline! I scarcely like to blame her; but when a girl sets herself against general rules, Heaven knows how it will end."

" In a convent, very likely," said some other friend of Madame Rendu.

Though they sat in judgment on them, all these people were glad to see the Rendus back again. Their gossip is to be taken only as one of the proofs that " man is the delight of man."

A great change was remarked in Pauline's appearance. Some thought it was an improvement, others that she was dreadfully gone off.

" You have grown, Pauline," said one madame.

" She looks so because she is thinner," remarked another.

" Remember, my dear," here put in Madame Chamband, " that youth does not last forever."

Even old Madame Jorey began to shoot arrows at her god-daughter; but that was after hearing that Pauline had refused M. Belair, the banker's only son.

On one of the Sunday visits, the old lady said more seriously than usual, " Pauline, when I was young, I had some of your rebellious spirit. I should have preferred another sort of husband to the one my father accepted for me. But Jorey did me the favor to live till I had reached the age of common sense, when I freely confessed my father had been right and I wrong. Depend on it, my child, customs which have ruled generation after generation are not without their *raison d'être.* Now, our custom from Adam has been to choose husbands and wives for our children; we know their dispositions, and what will suit them. Is an ignorant, unexperienced girl's fancy to rule her parents? Ridiculous!"

Pauline said quietly, " Do you think, then, that a girl's likings or dislikings ought to be overlooked?"

" She ought not to have any; a really good

girl should not know anything of feeling of preference as regards men."

" But suppose you cannot help having such feelings ? "

" Be ashamed of them, and conquer them, or they will lead you to perdition."

Pauline making no reply, the old lady uttered an impatient, " Well, little rebel ? "

" Indeed I am not rebellious."

" Just as Pharaoh said to Moses, and hardened his heart against all advice. Don't you understand that you are breaking God's commandment to honor and obey your father and mother ? Don't you see that you are committing the sin of putting self first ? Your mother is not half the woman she was ; she spares you, but you do not spare her. And if you had only a good cause ; but, my pretty one, you have but a very bad one. There, now I shall say no more."

Madame Jorey was not the woman to preach without a motive. In fact, St. Gloi was once more beginning to speculate as to Mademoiselle Rendu's marriage. It was in the air that another pretender was in the field. Rumor rivals M. Worth in the ingenious costumes it invents for whatever it has to drape ; in this instance it so travestied the one grain of fact, that it could never have been identified.

It was *said*—but that was nothing—it was actually *believed*, that Pauline was about to marry a black prince. The organist's wife shuddered, and exclaimed, " O heavens ? how glad I am I can go to the (organ) gallery. I would not miss seeing them married for gold. Horrible, isn't it?"

M. Léon Subar, the gentleman in question, possessed, indeed, a fine brown complexion, altogether different from African black. Though he had been born in Algiers, both parents were of unadulterated French blood. He was young, rich, handsome, and his own master, his father and mother being dead. He had met the Rendus at Aix les Bains, where they had stopped on their way homeward from Italy. He had danced with Pauline, heard her sing, was extremely struck by the beauty of her complexion and her lovely fair hair.

When M. Léon Subar wished to gratify himself, he was not wanting in energy. Now, as he had taken a fancy to make Pauline his wife, he speedily set in motion all the usual machinery by which matrimonial overtures are made. He procured an introduction to Madame Chambaud, through one of the many who knew of, or had heard of, that lady's especial talents, and he entrusted the negotiation to her.

Cool as Madame Rendu was, she was dazzled by the array of figures representing M. Subar's fortune.

"And so handsome into the bargain," observed Madame Chambaud in the tone of an auctioneer. .

"I don't believe Pauline has given him a

thought," sighed Madame Rendu. "I did
wrong not to marry her when she was eighteen."

"She will not have waited for nothing if she
becomes Madame Subar. It will be a magnificent marriage for her, and you really must
this time be firm. When the happiness of a
child is in the balance, it is a parent's duty
to—to tighten the reins." Madame Chambaud's metaphor halted, but not so her enthu.
siasm.

Madame Rendu said afterwards to M.
Rendu, as they talked the matter over, "How
easy other people's difficulties seem to us!"

Pauline understood perfectly that her dislike to marrying inflicted mortification and
pain on her parents. It was eccentric; and
nowhere in the world is eccentricity in a woman
so derided and condemned as in the small
provincial towns of France: it is considered
to denote a moral leprosy.

Hitherto Pauline, in right of her youth and
the Rendu fortune and position in St. Gloi,
had escaped this stigma. But indulgence and
patience have their limits. Many a time had
even Madame Rendu's iron nerves been jarred
by innuendoes as to the mystery of such and
such a girl of the speaker's acquaintance not
being married. But she dared not tell Pauline the reasons that might be invented to
account for her extraordinary obstinacy.

Pauline, however, was so lectured and advised on all hands, that she was brought to ask
herself "why she should refuse to do as others

did—it was evidently the rule to marry? Why then set herself against the rule? Why, indeed, save that she had more delicacy of feeling, more honesty of heart, than the generality; that she had a perception—dim, indeed, in reason of her inexperience—that marriage ought to be something better than a mere social contract and a union of fortunes?

# CHAPTER XVI.

*" Dans l'opinion du monde, la mariage, comme dans la comédie, finit tout. C'est précisement le contraire qui est vrai ; il commence tout."—Madame Sevetchine.*

THE next step was an interview between M. and Mme. Rendu and the " pretender." M. Subar was candor itself. He had nothing to conceal. He was " healthy, wealthy, and wise." That was his summing up of his qualifications. The address of his notary he offered. As for that of his medical man (quite in the usages to ask for it), he could not give it as— " *Mon Dieu!* I have never had one since I had the measles when I was six years old."

M. Subar was of course impatient for an answer. He did not dislike being the object of universal interest and observation in St. Gloi, but he would prefer being also assured that he was regarded as a conqueror, and not as a victim.

" My daughter cannot be hurried," replied Madame Rendu. At his gestures of vexation, she added, " It is for your sake I say so. It will not do to alarm her by pressing for an immediate decision."

M. Subar could scarcely conceal his surprise that any young lady could need time or preparation to say " Yes " to him. " Healthy,

wealthy, wise," and, " *ma foi, bel homme*,"
what could a girl want more ?

It had been one of Madame Rendu's frequently expressed self-laudations that she had
never felt timid under any circumstances—
that nothing ever threw her off her balance.
But what if her pulse had been felt when she
shut the door of her dressing-room on Pauline
and herself ?

Madame Rendu had this marriage at heart.
It was brilliant beyond her expectations. It
would be the happy *finale* to many anxieties
and mortifications endured in silence, and not
without a spice of heroism. Mingling with
all her commonplace views of life there was a
spark of the martyr's spirit which sacrifices all
for the sake of duty. No one could say
Madame Rendu had swerved an iota from her
idea of the straight line. An obedient daughter, she had married M. Rendu, not only indifferent to him, but with a suspicion of aversion. She had been a steady matron, strict in
conduct if not affectionate in manner, and a con-
scientious mother. Naturally, she expected
that her daughter could do what she had done.
Madame Rendu did not believe in any stronger
feelings than her own, measuring (as indeed
we all do) others by herself.

Pauline turned very pale when her mother
opened the conversation by saying, " I have
something serious to talk to you about."

Pauline kissed her mother before taking the
chair by her side.

"I am quite prepared, mamma, for your information." This was spoken with a little nervous laugh.

Madame Rendu did not approve of this taking of the initiative out of her hands; it augured ill for the success of M. Subar's proposal, at all events.

"My dear, hear what I have to say before giving me an answer."

Pauline listened as silent and motionless as if she had been a statue to an enumeration of all the advantages, personal and material, to be gained through becoming M. Subar's wife. This was followed by an outburst of long pent-up disappointment. Madame Rendu warming up into something like eloquence as she spoke of her own thwarted expectations, and of the small gratitude Pauline had shown for all the care and kindness lavished on her. In truth, Madame Rendu, in her dread of a new failure, said more than she meant or than was true. Pauline's demeanor remained as calm under this avalanche of reproach as she had done under the glowing picture of M. Subar as a husband.

Madame Rendu wound up by saying, "I know you have some absurd theory about loving the man you marry. That means just this—you love your own fancy. No woman ever sees what a man really is till after marriage."

"Such reasoning, dear mother, goes to prove that it is as well to take one man as another.

That being so, I will accept of M. Subar as my future husband."

This unexpected acquiescence startled Madame Rendu. Her first speech showed this, being so contradictory of what she had been trying to impress on Pauline.

"Of course, if you feel a repugnance to this gentleman."

"Not more for him than another. As I must marry, it is lucky that I can please you and my father."

Madame Rendu did not, after all, relish this mode of acceptance, though it had in it many of the usual words with which young ladies announce their consent. She would have liked to put the crucial question, " Would you have made exactly this answer had it, instead of M. Subar, been M. Vilpont," but she dared not.

Not half so pleased as the fulfilment of her wish should have made her, Madame Rendu wrote to invite M. Subar to dinner next day.

He understood that the invitation meant acceptance.

He was received in the *grand salon* by his future father and mother in law. Then Pauline was summoned, and asked by her father if she willingly accepted M. Leon Subar for her husband. She bowed, and M. Rendu added solemnly, " M. Subar, embrace your wife."

Leon sprang forward, kissed Pauline first on both cheeks, and then her two hands. Turning from her to her parents, he received the paternal and maternal *accolade*. After that

they went in to dinner, which saved the awk-
wardness of the situation. Before evening
the event was known to half the town, discussed at the *Circle*, and was the one subject
of conversation in most of the drawing-rooms.

"Really I can scarcely believe it," said Stephanie de Saye. " Pauline had got quite an
old-maid look, and yet M. Subar is—so Madame Chambaud says—wild about her."

Nothing could be more graceful, more according to etiquette, than Pauline's behavior
during two days. She sat by the side of her
betrothed, sang and played at his request,
smiled when he spoke to her ; yet before the
end of the third day Léon was exasperated
and despairing.

" She was so charming at Aix, and now she
is like a machine. I wonder if it's her mother's fault."

Pauline was every whit as uneasy and distressed.

Imagine Madame Rendu's feelings when
Pauline suddenly asked her if she could not
withdraw her word.

" Do you want to break my heart ? " asked
the dismayed mother, and left the room in a
paroxysm of alarm.

What was to be the end of it all ? It had been
trying to have a daughter averse to marry—
painful to believe that this aversion had given
rise to disagreeable surmises. But what was
that to the inevitable results of Pauline's breaking her word to M. Subar ? The poor lady

could not and did not conceal from herself that nothing less would happen than that there would be waggings of heads and sage observations that there must be *some* cause for such extraordinary conduct. Madame Rendu seemed to hear shrill voices pronouncing adverse verdicts—"Such a handsome, agreeable, rich, young man—a very *beau idéal* of a husband—to be refused! There must be a cause; and what was it?"

Madame Rendu was as sure of these remarks being made as though she actually heard them. She had a clue to Pauline's reluctance, but others had not, and she hoped, with all her heart, they never might find it. "Oh, that man! that man! Ugly, too; and M. Subar so superior in so many ways!" It was useless now to give way to regret, it was necessary to act, to get some help with this terribly uncommon girl. In her dire strait, Madame Rendu sent for Madame Chambaud.

Madame Chambaud hurried in all smiles, and began a string of commonplace congratulations.

"So handsome, so pleasant, so rich. Really it did always so happen; riches went as naturally to riches as rivers to the sea. But where, then, was the young madame?"

"Yes," returned Madame Rendu; "he is rich, handsome, and amiable. But Pauline never can be like other people, I now believe Madame Agnes put every kind of crotchet into her silly little head. She is in bed to-day.

One would suppose no one had ever been married before."

" And the handsomest man I have seen these twenty years !" ejaculated plaintively Madame Chambaud.

" Yesterday she was all cheerfulness," went on Madame Rendu; "and now there she is, her face hid in her pillow."

" Let me go to her, dear madame; I have had some experience of these girlish panics," said Madame Chambaud, and with truth. " Some need scolding, some coaxing, but I always managed to cure their terrors."

Madame Chambaud was not the least daunted by Pauline's face or her wide-opened pathetic eyes. She sat herself down by the bedside, and delivered quite an oration on M. Subar's good looks and other advantages. " Pauline, you are born to be lucky. You go on refusing most eligible offers, and just when one fears you will have to accept the crooked stick, behold the lovely young prince, a real Fortunatus, falls at your feet and bestows on you all that woman's heart can desire. My dear, I congratulate you with all my heart. The whole town, I assure you, is full of wonder and delight. You really are an honor to St. Gloi; and then, how happy your father and mother are. It's delightful !" Here another look at the colorless face with the large eyes made her add, " Of course, you are a little nervous. One always is after pronouncing the great ' yes.' I was nervous myself, so I can understand your feelings. I always liken marriage to death—though it takes us into a better world it frightens us."

And so on rattled Madame Chambaud, taking everything for granted, reiterating always, that everybody felt alike on such occasions, and that every one was happier afterwards in proportion to their previous reluctance.

Pauline turned away from the proffered embrace, praying earnestly for patience. Not from any Madame Chambaud could she have asked help. What was done could not be re-called, save at the expense of a public scandal, which would break the heart of her parents. So she submitted.

Léon tried the patience she prayed for to the utmost. He was a terrible lover. Demonstrative to a degree that scandalized all the elderly ladies and set all the old gentlemen grinning, he was a source of infinite wonder and interest to all the young girls.

Luckily Pauline's trial was shortened by his being obliged to go to Paris on business. Before his departure, however, the day for the marriage was fixed, and a tour to the Oberland planned to fill up the time while their hotel in Paris was being furnished.

An hotel in Paris! How the St. Gloisians *Ah!*'d, and *Ciel*'d, and *Ma foi*'d; and how they repeated those significant sounds when the *corbeille* presented by Léon arrived. "Diamonds and rubies fit for a queen! You might set up a jeweller's shop, *ma chérie!*"

exclaimed Madame de Saye, almost going down on her knees to the trinkets.

Never either had such a trousseau been even imagined in St. Gloi. Madame Rendu had sent for everything from Paris. Some feeling made her lavish in all that money could buy for Pauline.

Madame de Saye forced her husband to write an account of the marriage to M. Vilpont de Kergeac. " Remember, darling, to mention that the bride's dress cost five thousand francs, and that she wore a profusion of diamonds. Oh, and the mayor's speech! Do put that in."

The mayor had said everything possible to be said in praise of bridegroom, bride, and bride's parents. He had concluded thus :—

" *Mesdames et Messieurs*, I may now say, with our inimitable Beranger,* ' I have seen Peace descend upon the earth, sowing corn, flowers, and gold.' "

Many elbows had met significantly at this announcement.

" So appropriate ! " observed Madame Chambaud.

---

* "J'ai vu la Paix descendre sur la terre,
    Semant de l'or, des fleurs, et des épis."

7

# PART II.

# CHAPTER I.

## A DOMESTIC TREASURE.

Léon and his wife travelling to Paris on a fine October day, were within half-an-hour of arrival at their destination, when after an unusually long silence he said, " I hope you will be pleased with your new home, and my arrangements about servants."

" I have no doubts on that point," replied Pauline; " but I am rather frightened at the idea of having to manage Paris servants. I only understand St. Gloi ways of housekeeping."

" Ah! I had some idea you would not know how to manage, so I sent for my foster sister and her husband, and they will take all trouble off your hands. Zelic was brought up by my mother; she can do anything and everything, and has such pleasant ways; always cheerful and good-tempered—a real treasure."

" You cannot think what a load of anxiety you have taken from me. And what is Joseph, her husband; coachman or footman?"

" Oh! Joseph is an excellent fellow, honesty itself, but not clever like Zelic; in fact, rather limited as to talent, what we call *un bon sot*.

But he will make a very good major-domo
under his wife's direction. Between them you
will have nothing to do but amuse yourself."

"How kind of you to arrange all this," said
Pauline, feeling really grateful; "I wish you
had told mamma; she has been fretting as to
how I should get on."

Léon did not speak his thoughts when he
answered, "The information will come better
from you, when you can say you like Zelie."
Had he been in the Palace of Truth he would
have said, "Your mother, my dear, would have
filled your little head with warnings and suspicions, and probably would have gratified me
with a visit fruitful of investigations."

Nothing could look more cheerful to a
young wife's eye than her new home did to
Pauline. Great gates opened on a court-
yard, the carriage-drive was round a small lawn
as soft as velvet, and green as an emerald,
thanks to the *jet d'eau* throwing constantly
across it what glistened like diamond dust.

On each side of the double flight of steps
leading to the *perron* was a dazzle of
autumn flowers in porcelain vases. As the
carriage drove in, a man ran down the steps
dressed like a gentleman, and Pauline supposed he was some friend come to welcome
them, until she heard her husband say, "How
are you, Joseph?" Joseph was well, and
hoped Madame was not too tired.

A tall woman waited on the *perron*, she
made a graceful curtsey to Madame Subar, who

putting out her hand said, " M. Subar has been talking to me of his good foster sister."

Zelie scarcely touched the kind little hand.

Léon's greeting of Zelie surprised Pauline. " *Eh! bien mon enfant comment cela va-t-il,*" and he kissed her on both cheeks.

" Now take charge of madame," he added, with an odd laugh. Had Madame Rendu been present, she would have judged that Léon was something afraid of his foster sister.

" Madame will give herself the trouble to follow me," said Zelie; and mistress and servant went up the wide staircase, the last first and the first last. " Madame I hope finds her room to her taste."

" It is beautiful! how could I help liking it. But Zelie, I shall call you Zelie as Léon does, you had better desire Marie, my maid, to come up. You are Madame la Gouvernante, you know."

" Permit me, madame, to assist you to-day, always if you please. I have been trained to all the duties of a lady's-maid."

" Well, just for this once ; but poor Marie would not like to be put on one side."

Nothing could be more unexceptionable than Zelie's words, nor more deft than her services ; but Pauline, nevertheless, longed for the sight of Marie's broad face, and the help given by hands that touched her always respectfully as well as with kindliness.

Zelie's opinion of the new madame was not favorable. She said afterwards to Joseph,

" What in the name of all the saints did he see in her, to make him marry her ? "

" She is pretty, like a white dove," replied simple Joseph.

" You may as well say like a sheep or a white rabbit, or milk or any white thing ; but she has no style, no figure ; there's nothing of her, and such amiability ! Zelie this and Zelie that, as if she wanted to encourage me."

Joseph shrugged his shoulders pacifically, and said : " I dare say she means well ; better try and put up with her. She will let you do as you please."

" If she had been a magnificent creature, with the air of a queen," went on Zelie, unheeding of Joseph's counsel, " I could have worshipped her, but this scrap of a woman, half a woman, I call her."

" Well, well, it was his fancy, and she is not to blame for that, nor her smallness either, and she is pretty, poor thing ! "

" Joseph, you are an ass ; enough to drive one mad with your way of being satisfied with everything. I tell you Léon has thrown himself away ; it is *he* who is to be pitied."

Zelie was no beauty herself. She was a woman of thirty, at the least, of a dark complexion, with strange eyes—eyes the color of the sea when it is neither green nor blue, but with something of both colors. They were expressive eyes, that could sparkle fiercely and darken with tenderness. At first sight you called her plain, but no one kept that opinion

long.  She had some indefinable attraction
which had made many conquests.  When Léon
was twenty he was desperately in love with
her, and would have married her, could he
have gained the consent of his parents.  How
she had condescended at last to take Joseph
for her spouse, does not enter into Pauline's
history.  The only point necessary to mention
is, that she had obtained a promise from Léon
that she and Joseph should always form part
of his household.

By the end of November the Subars were in
the full current of Paris gayety.  Pauline had
her box at the *Italiens*, her share of one at the
Grand Opera—she went for all first represen-
tations—her *coupé* and horses were perfect of
their kind; and, in two words, she lived the
life of a rich idle woman, as did Léon that of
a rich idle man.

When the first gloss of novelty had vanished,
the feelings of the provincial woman began to
reassert themselves.  *N'est pas Parisienne,
qui veut*, and Pauline had been accustomed to
a circle of intimates.  She had known, by
sight, at least, every creature in St. Gloi; their
births, deaths, and marriages had been matters
of interest.  She had had a round of duties to
perform—she had known herself of some
importance in different ways to her neighbors.
But there was nothing of this sort to give zest
to her life in Paris.  She was nothing beyond
a drop of water in the ocean.

No one who has not been uprooted from

among familiar faces, scenes and occupations, all grown into a part of one's self, can sympathize with Pauline's growing *ennui* in her fine house, or in her smart carriage. She would have willingly resigned both to be again trotting to the *ouvroir* along the ill-paved streets of St. Gloi; to be again cutting out shirts and petticoats to the accompaniment of a small stream of local gossip, or to be making *bonbons* under the superintendence of the old godmother.

Many a quiet cry she had over old days. It seemed to her as if she were gradually stupefying, caring for nothing and nobody. Something in her letters must have betrayed her depression to her mother and Madame Agnes; the one wrote recommending her to be active in good works, and vigilant in performing her religious duties,—the other urging her to keep up her music and all her other accomplishments. "You appear," wrote Madame Rendu, "to have given up all your studies, as though your education had cost nothing."

Léon, who read all his wife's letters, here remarked, "I thank God you *have* given them up."

Madame Rendu went on: "You do not seem to me to order your life, so as to fulfil gracefully all your duties."

Léon stopped short—"Ha! You go regularly to mass, don't you, little one; and to confession and all that" (he never did himself). "I should not approve of any neglect of that kind." he added, with the austere air of a judge. "A woman without religion is not pleasant as a man's wife."

Pauline said, "I assure you, Léon, I never neglect any religious duty. Mamma means, I suppose, that I don't practise enough."

"Hang the piano," said Léon.

"Or perhaps she fancies I don't attend to the house; she thinks I ought to be my own housekeeper."

"But you prefer to have Zelie, don't you?"

"Oh! I don't know what I should do without her; she saves me even the trouble of thinking about my dress."

"Then what do you think about?" asked Léon, with sudden curiosity.

"I have not much time for thought, have I? I do nothing, and yet I never have any time to spare."

"You'll have plenty when Lent comes; now *sans* adieu! my kitten. I have an appointment, and must be off."

Léon and Pauline were on very friendly terms, but the period of lively demonstrations on his part had been, and was gone. *Parlez moi des neiges d'autan.*

Léon still, as a rule, breakfasted with his wife, and dined at home when they had no engagement. But in other respects he was leading what the French call *la vie Parisienne* —that is, he was caught in the gear of a monstrous machine which grinds to dust the souls and hearts, bodies and fortunes of men.

Léon was in the habit of boasting about his
wife; of how well he had managed to train
her, that she let him do as he liked—never in-
terfering with any of his pleasures.

Old experienced men smiled at his *naïveté*,
while congratulating him on the possession of
such a pearl. They accounted for Pauline's
perfection of temper as arising either from indifference or from her having some compensation which Léon was ignorant of. Difficult
for hardened and long-sighted men of the
world to be charitable in their judgments. In
short, Pauline's purity and childlike unsus-
piciousness was simply incredible to those who
knew she was by no means an idiot.

Zelie, too, who saw her so closely, was puzzled. Always so good, as if she could not see
the wickedness all round her. Was she a
hypocrite or a saint? The perversities of poor
human nature are puzzling. Why did Zelie,
knowing her goodness, hate Pauline? and
hate her with that most formidable of hatreds
—a gratuitous hate?

It forces one to believe that, as love exists
of itself, so does hatred. Love ceases, indeed,
unless fed; but hatred feeds on itself and
thrives. Love often dies; hate, alas! seldom.

Léon had resumed all the old familiarity of
his boyish days with Zelie, and had asked
Zelie what she thought of his wife.

And Zelie had made him understand clearly
enough, that she saw nothing in Pauline to
account for a man so handsome and rich hav-

ing married her. Léon, stupid enough to discuss his wife with her servant, was naturally
stupid enough to be influenced by the servant's
opinion. Many a half-hour he now spent in
the housekeeper's parlor, listening to all the
gossip and scandal Zelie was assiduous in
scraping together for his amusement. Her
highly spiced anecdotes came to be more agreeable to him than his wife's conversation. He
began himself to wonder at his former infatu-
ation about Pauline.

It must be allowed that Madame Léon Subar
was not what Mademoiselle Pauline Rendu
had been. Madame Subar had none of Pauline's playfulness; all her girlish waywardness
and innocent piquancy had disappeared. She
was perfectly good and obedient, but not unlike unrippled water, reflecting serenely everything, and having no individuality.

Pauline was not blind to Léon's growing indifference. With her usual tendency to self-
depreciation, she said to herself, " I am no
better than I used to be—growing worse, I
believe, for I make no return for all the
pleasures bestowed on me. Do all people
grow tired of being well off, of having no
troubles ? "

Pauline had not yet come to understand that
the greatest of all troubles is an empty heart.

# CHAPTER II.

### STEPHANIE'S DISCOVERIES.

AT this moment all the energies of the upper world of Paris were concentrated on canvassing for seats at the " Deux Etoiles " Theatre, for the first representation of a new play by Alberic Vilpont. Ministers, ambassadors, the press, actors, actresses, and above all, the author himself, were attacked with every possible weapon. Husbands were snubbed or coaxed ; those who failed in their exertions were ill-used and trampled on. Wearied-out managers and box-keepers swore in vain that every seat in the house had been secured for the first ten nights before even an announcement of the performance had appeared. There was one exception to this *furore* of curiosity —Pauline had not spoken to Léon on the subject. She was not quite sure that she wished to see the play, or that it would be right in her to have such a wish. Her conscientiousness was perhaps exaggerated, but she desired to avoid having thoughts she would not willingly impart to her husband—disloyalty was of all things that she most dreaded and scorned. On the very morning of the day of the first representation of " Un bon Mariage," Madame de Saye rushed into the dining-room where the Subars were at breakfast.

Giving Pauline a hasty kiss, Stephanie seated herself by M. Subar, saying, "How lucky to find you at table; I am dying of hunger! Gaston has gone to M. Vilpont—we want places for to-night. After our coming all this way on purpose for his play he cannot refuse us, and such an old friend, too, as Gaston. It is to be quite an event."

"I doubt if even M. Vilpont can give you seats. I have only been able to secure one stall for myself," returned Léon, not quite pleased at being thus taken by storm.

M. Subar was one of those unfortunates who can never have intimates—he was too fond of display to be friendly. He understood by hospitality overwhelmingly grand dinners. He shrank from anything like the familiarity which says, "Oh! come in, and take what is going."

Stephanie, who, to do her justice, cared little how she appeased her hunger, went on, turning to Pauline: "If I had been you, I would have written at once to M. Vilpont. He would never have refused *you* anything." Then with still happier tact she added, "You would not have been jealous, would you, M. Subar?"

Léon laid down his knife and fork, and gaped.

"I am not," continued the chatterbox, "though M. de Saye did make an offer to Pauline before he proposed to me."

"Why, what can this M. Vilpont have to do with Madame Subar or with me?" asked Léon, with a high and mighty air, which made Stephanie laugh.

"Oh! my dear sir, don't be offended: the gentleman we call M. Vilpont is really the Vicomte de Kergeac, and will be a marquis some day. Is his uncle dead?" she added, turning to Pauline.

"I have heard nothing about M. Vilpont since he left St. Gloi," replied Pauline.

"I suppose he is offended with you," remarked Stephanie.

"What are you talking about?" asked Léon.

"I had always believed," said Pauline with a gravity that suppressed Stephanie for the time, "it was scarcely honorable to tell such things; but the matter is simple enough, Léon —M. Vilpont honored me by a proposal of marriage, which my father declined."     .

"Why, if he is really a man of rank."

"That, I fancy, was one of the reasons; my mother thought it might separate me from my own relations. But indeed, Léon, I know very little about the matter, as I was not consulted."

"And if you had been?"

"I should have done as my parents advised."

"I see I had better have held my tongue," said Stephanie.

"I think so," answered Pauline calmly.

"I tell Gaston everything—everything; so I thought, of course, you did the same."

"Pauline is not so frank, as you may perceive," said Léon sulkily.

It was not quite true that Stephanie bore no

grudge to Pauline on account of the offer M.
de Saye had made her; but though she had
many petty feelings, Madame de Saye was not
really ill-intentioned; so now she set to work
to put Léon into good-humor again. She had
one decided talent, that of coaxing; and so,
what with her prettiness, her little flattering,
and her silliness, Léon's brow lost its ruffle, and
his pouting lips were once more able to smile
when Gaston came in.

"Have you got places?" shrieked Stephanie,
flying to him.

"I am starving, my dear."

"Answer first," went on Stephanie. "Now
don't tease; you know I hate to be kept in
suspense." All the time her fingers were busy
diving into his waistcoat and coat pockets, he
standing still, as if he liked the process.

"I declare I believe you have not got any.
It's very ill-natured of M. Vilpont, after all
the kindness he received at St. Gloi;" and Stephanie sat down ready to cry.

Her husband, now at liberty, made his salutations to M. and Mme. Subar, and took the
offered seat at table.

"Pauline has got no place either," observed
Stephanie.

"I am happy we have it in our power to
rectify that misfortune—there, you spiteful little puss," and Gaston threw the *coupon* of a
box into her lap.

She exclaimed, "Only think! *an avant
scène*, close to the stage. We shall be as well

placed as any princess. I never did have an
*avant scène,* even when I was first married."

"I shall keep to my stall," said Léon, with a
dignity lost on his audience.

It was a matter of course that the De Sayes
should be invited to dinner, which Léon resolved should be one the provincials could not
easily forget.

Being in high good-humor, Stephanie went
into raptures over the house and furniture, and
said so often, "O you lucky girl, Pauline!
what could you wish for more?" that Léon remarked afterwards (what had never before
been said of Stephanie) that Madame de Saye
was really a clever woman.

"I have set everything to rights, haven't I,
Pauline?" asked Stephanie, as soon as they
had been left *tête-à-tête.* She was standing in
front of a mirror as she said this.

"What was there to set to rights?"

"O Pauline! are you blind?—my hair."

"It's as smooth as glass."

"And my *paniers,* are they straight? I
have not been near a glass till now since we
arrived."

"You look as if you had come out of a band-
box."

Stephanie left the mirror, and suddenly
throwing her arms round Pauline, whispered,
as she held her in a tight embrace, "Take care
what you say, some one is listening." Without waiting for any reply, she then dashed into
discussions of the fashions, wondering whether

covering her forehead with little curls, or frizzing her hair into a shapeless confusion, would become her best.

" You have told me nothing about my godson," said Pauline.

"How easily one forgets," laughed Stephanie. "I do not mean, my boy, but that there ever was a time when I was not married. Strange enough, but quite true. Oh! Bébé is a handsome, beautiful boy, and he is beginning to talk; Gaston cannot make out what he says, but I always can. He calls his papa Bob, because he hears him calling to his dog—Bob. Mamma is taking care of Bébé. She did not like Gaston coming to Paris without me. Don't you wish you had a Bébé too—a girl would suit you best, and then our children could marry."

"If ever I have children, they shall choose for themselves," said Pauline.

"Mine shall not," retorted Stephanie stoutly. "No, I shall stick to the good old rules."

"Have you no shopping to do; nowhere you would wish to go?" asked Pauline, in order to change the subject.

"I have heaps of commissions for mamma; but if I shop in your fine carriage, I shall have to pay double. Let us go by and by to the Bois."

During the drive Stephanie said, " You remember what I said to you about my hair; that was all a *ruse*. You must be on your guard, Pauline; that brown woman is a spy. I would send her away as soon as possible."

"My dear Stephanie, are you dreaming?"

"On the contrary, quite awake. I know I never was so clever as you and Julie, but I have very good eyes."

"What have you seen?"

"I turned off what I was going to say, asking you about my hair, because I caught sight of that woman behind the door. I saw her in the glass as distinctly as I now see you. She was still there when I sat down by you on the sofa."

"Zelie is quite above such conduct; and why should she listen?"

"I don't know, indeed. As for her being above it, that's absurd; all servants are spies. I would not have her in the house a day; she blinks her eyes like a cat."

"As for sending her away, I should need a very good reason. She is Léon's foster-sister, and he is very much attached to her."

"That would be reason enough for me. Why don't you ask your mother to interfere?"

"I will never ask mamma to come between me and my husband, and for what, very likely, is a mistake of yours."

"Very well; I felt it was my duty to warn you. Don't blame me if yellow-face steals your diamonds or murders you one of these days; it would not astonish me."

"It would me," said Pauline, laughing.

Nevertheless Pauline, while dressing for the evening, did take more notice than usual of Zelie's ways. Hitherto she had rather tried to like Léon's foster-sister than really done so.

She now admitted to herself that the manners and looks of her lady's-maid were unpleasant and distasteful. She shrugged her shoulders far too familiarly when Pauline refused to cold-cream and powder her face.

"Madame will look swarthy in the light of the theatre. It is always most unbecoming to blondes. Madame ought to wish to do honor to monsieur."

"My good Zelie, if monsieur chose me as I am, is it not honoring him to keep the same face?"

"As madame pleases."

Léon tapped at the door, and on Zelie opening it, said, "Tell my wife she must wear her diamonds. It is a first representation, and all the women will be in gala."

"But if Stephanie has not brought hers, she will not like my wearing mine," remonstrated Pauline.

"What's that to you? Here, Zelie, bring me the box. I shall show that Monsieur Chose* you have something more than his empty title. He is as poor as a rat—De Saye told me so; lives by his wits, poor devil!"

Léon took the jewels out of their cases, spreading them out lovingly on the toilet-table. He chose a *rivière*, bracelets, earrings, and a sort of semi-circlet for the head.

"Not that," said Pauline; "it always makes my head ache."

* Thing—as common an expression in France as *Thing a mee* in England.

"That's nonsense," said Léon. "However, I will be satisfied with the butterfly; put it where it will be well seen, Zelie."

"I suppose I may lend these two little stars to Stephanie?" asked Pauline.

"Tell her to take care of them," said Léon.

When the diamonds were all placed, Léon said, "Now give me a kiss, such pretty things are worth more than that. How pale you are," he added.

"I have already made that observation to madame," said Zelie.

"You should let Zelie put a touch of *rouge* under your eyes," said Léon.

"I shall have color enough in that hot theatre," said Pauline.

She carried the diamond stars to Stephanie, saying, "You must wear these to keep me in countenance."

"With the best will in the world," was the answer. "O, Pauline, what a lucky girl you are!" an observation made for at least the tenth time that day. "If only some of our own set from St. Gloi could see us, I should not have anything left to wish for. I never was so happy in my life."

It was so pleasant to witness Stephanie's delight, that the three others petted and admired her as though she had done some good deed. There was evidently a virtue in her pleasure by the friendly feeling it diffused among them.

"What a number of carriages!" exclaimed

the little woman as they came near the theatre; and she pinched her husband's arm till he cried out for mercy.

But in Paris people of all ranks behave decently in a crowd. They do not hit out or jostle women to get one minute sooner to their places. So M. de Saye conducted his two companions to their box without any ruffle to their hair or their dress.

Léon went to his stall, because he had said he would, and repented at leisure of his haste in speech.

## CHAPTER III.

### A FRENCH PLAY.

THE house was crammed to the roof—the very galleries filled by men of talent and education.

"I wonder where M. Vilpont is?" exclaimed Madame de Saye, using her opera-glass energetically. "Hid away in some corner. I did not tell you before, but we have got his box. If the piece is successful, he will be called for."

Pauline sat in one corner, sheltered by a curtain. Her heart was beating in a way she could not understand, as if she had been the author of the play herself. She might have said or sung with Zerlina, "*Vorrei e non vorrei.*" She wished, and did not wish, to see M. Vilpont.

The curtain rose, and in an instant there was a general hush of expectation.

It was the first representation of a great comedy. Whatever else decayed, the stage flourished under Napoleon. Augier, Feuillet, and Sardou, wrote as no French authors have written since Molière, and Vilpont was acknowledged as their equal. The corruption of society afforded the playwright ample matter for scathing satire; the taste for sensuous fairy pieces and coarse buffooneries concentrated the few good actors the age could produce in one or two theatres. The system of election at the Français, though tampered with by the Court, still culled the very flower of the talent of France; the prevalent luxury allowed the actresses to rival the great ladies of the Court in the magnificence of their dress; the long practice of the audience, who had seen plays from their childhood, and their utter want of faith in anything (even in the " Ma Mère," which used to bring down the house), kept the actor and author from leaving, by one hair's-breadth, the path of true feeling for the seductive bogs of exaggeration or maudlin sentiment; while admission to the Academy, the highest distinction a literary Frenchman can gain, was only to be earned by the playwright if his style could bear cold-blooded criticism applied in the closet by trained anatomists who enjoyed vivisection. No actor, no actress, however popular, was safe from that malignant howl of derision which greets a failure in tone, expression, or gesture, and which makes an Englishman's blood boil, however fully, as a critic, he may agree with the disapprobation so brutally expressed.

Owing to these causes, Pauline saw what few men or women out of Paris ever saw—a great play perfectly acted.

The subject of the play was "Marriage." In a few scenes Vilpont presented many of the views held in France concerning this much-betalked institution. There was the *ingénue*

8

—pure, naïve, ignorant, inclined in a feeble
way to fall in love with the good young man,
but rather likely also to fall an easy victim to
the practised *roué*. The girl was full of
pretty little aspirations, with a perfume of
daisies and hay about them, but was also
keenly alive to the anticipated pleasures of
the Bois, the opera, and the ball-room. Her
dress was simplicity itself, her eyes all candor, her voice artless; and yet you felt that
she too, if married to the wrong rich man,
would develop into a splendid creature very
like the true heroine of the play, the married
woman of ten years' standing. How beautiful
she was! With what exquisite grace the full
form and haughty figure lounged on the
stage, wreathed in the richest silks, the most
costly lace! How every murmur of the low
voice told of passion, a passion beyond silks
and lace, the passion of French flesh and
blood.

Then there was the old woman—past passion
for aught but herself, loving even her children
only for herself, admiring the ingenuous girl
with a real belief that innocence was quite
right at seventeen, but not a thing to be much
wished for afterwards, especially as repentance
could be made very pleasant at fifty, with the
aid of a *roué* marquis and a fashionable abbé.

Then the men. There was the good young
man—an engineer, very wise, very gentle, not
too poor, who said the prettiest things about
love and virtue, but was in sad danger when

left much alone with the practised coquette of thirty. Without this foible the audience could not have stood him. Then there was the true hero, the "*grand premier*," madly in love with the married woman, and bound by every tie of honor and affection to her husband. He had been terribly wicked, and was destined for the *ingénue ;* but such a marriage the audience felt would end in her destruction, and in his sinking to still more awful gulfs of vice. His only chance of good conduct in this world, and salvation in the next, lay in running away with his friend's wife, if this could be done with propriety, and here was *the* crux of the play.

Then we had the old philosopher—poor, gray-headed, wild-eyed; a republican, *pur sang,* incapable of baseness, who disbelieved in marriage altogether, but was the only man in the play free from vice, only he had been venal in his day, having sold his pen, and now, aspiring philosophically towards a virtue of his own, which happened to be incompatible with venality, he did not like the consequences.

Now for the husband—rich, addicted to the club, the bourse, and quiet, but expensive, infidelity. His general unpleasantness was redeemed only by courtesy and liberality to his wife, and real kindness to her would-be seducer; he despised the philosopher, and made use of him. Next the *roué* marquis, no better than the rest, but

able to say very witty things, pointing out the
advantages of outward decency and good
manners over the impudent, bad manners of
the *parvenus ;* add a creature in black standing for a priest, although the *" Censure"*
would not let him be called one, and you have
the *dramatis personæ.*

Was the pure-hearted child to become the
worldly woman? Was the little flicker of
true love to be fed with wholesome fuel until
it should burn clear on a happy hearth, sur-
rounded by loved children and an honored
husband? Or was a cruel system to quench
this flame, leaving only a smouldering spark
hereafter to burst out in a conflagration of
passion such as was consuming that other
glorious creature, by whose side the gentle
woes of the little *ingénue* paled into insignifi-
cance? How that poor married woman of
thirty wound herself into your heart as you
gazed on the scene! Were not her faults, her
extravagance, her love of admiration, her love
of men's love, the faults of society? Were
not her merits, her passionate heart, her contempt for the finery around her, her longing
for real life, real duties, all her own? How
could she love that husband? How could so
ardent a being live without love? And yet
she clung to duty, and, in defiance of nature,
of sin all round her, of a husband's infidelity,
she *would* remain pure and true, *if* only the
temptation did not become too strong. So
passionate, so natural was the love she felt,

that the audience trembled as they saw her
tempest-tossed, hardly knowing whether they
wished her to yield or to be true—to be true
to her vows or to nature.

But there stood the elder woman. She had
yielded, had been true to nature once in her
life, and a terrible beacon she was, warning
womankind from the lie that looked like
truth. In days gone by she had succumbed
to passion, and, as the world counts, had lost
nothing. She was honored and rich, but she
had lost what neither honor nor riches can give
—she had lost all faith in truth and goodness;
she believed nothing, hoped nothing, forgave
nothing. Her husband had been to her a
species of necessary disease somewhat analo-
gous to vaccination. The lover of her youth
had convinced her that the ideal man, when
he proffered love, meant to consume a woman
as he would a partridge; that the devotion of
man to woman was a mere bait to lure the
victim. Her own heart said that woman was
no better than man; and the one law left her
was to seek her own interest with prudence,
the only difficulty being to find anything remaining in the world that could give her grati-
fication. The one thing she was sure of was
that her own education had been perfect, and
the system which had produced *her* the best
possible. Unfortunately, the dead sins of her
youth had left ghosts, which most inconveni-
ently interfered with her present case.

Round this nice set the marquis and the

philosopher hovered complacently, helping the
drama forward, and stating the views of the
old *régime* and coming commune on the actual state of social relations in France.

This is the dry analysis of a somewhat unfriendly critic; but had you been there,
reader, you would have done what the audience did. The tears would have stood in your
eyes at the spectacle of the gentle girl, so unconscious of her peril on the edge of the terrible vortex, whirling the main protagonists to
death and misery. In breathless suspense you
would have hung on every passionate word of
that poor man and woman—now lost, now
saved, now lost. The commonplace husband,
by dint of sheer reality, would have wrung
your heart. Why should he suffer so, merely
because he was commonplace? Your heart
would have burned with wrath at the witty
egotism of the old woman and her marquis;
you would have believed for a moment the
wild theories of the philosopher; anything
would have seemed better to you than a system which produced such ills. When the play
began, you would have laughed till the tears
ran down your cheeks at the humor with
which each character displayed its foibles;
and at the end, you would have forgotten
theories, characters, actors, audience, your
friends, your tears, your very existence, in
breathless agony at the misery you saw and
could not help. Then you would have shouted
and clapped and stamped, and stood up and

roared for Vilpont, as though he had been a demigod who had saved mankind by satire, instead of a man with no reform to suggest, who lashed with dexterous whip a little section of the dumb abstraction called society.

The audience did all this, and with dry mouths and still wet eyes, as they went home basked in the self-approving glow they felt at having so thoroughly sympathized in all the good sentiments and execrated all the bad feelings. They had exercised the best part of their natures at the cost of a few francs, and next day they were no more disposed to alter their practice than the coldest British audience that ever smiled a dignified approval at stale platitudes about the sin of loving money and worshipping the aristocracy. Pauline saw it all, and saw how far she had come upon the path.

# CHAPTER IV.

### PAINFUL REALITIES.

ALL in vain did Pauline say to herself that M. Vilpont had used the lash, not against any individual case, but against the general custom as to marriage in France. After all, was it very sure that any better way could be devised? Was it not constantly said that there were as many ill-assorted couples in those countries where love-matches were the rule? All her arguments were impotent; she was wounded —sorely wounded.

For nine days the subject of the play was discussed in every *salon* and in every newspaper. The question of marriage was handled poetically, philosophically, and practically; from men's point of view, from that of young women and middle-aged women. The old contented themselves with a smile, accompanied by a mysterious shake of the head; they had given up the problem long ago. The mothers were to a woman in favor of the old custom. The play and the discussions were both withheld from young girls.

At the end of nine days came a scrawl from Stephanie, to which there was this *P. S.*—

"I saw your friend M. Vilpont before we left Paris, and I gave him a good scolding for not having been to call on you. I told him you would like to see him; because I know you would, though you did not tell me so."

This news caused Pauline no little anxiety. She first wondered if Vilpont would come— she hoped he would not; it would be awkward. It was five years since that memorable day in the vineyard—five years! Time enough to have had another deluge and repeopling of the world; but Pauline was inexperienced, and had not mastered the fact that she was not the same person she had been at nineteen, and *ergo*, M. Vilpont would probably meet her with amiable indifference. It is always with difficulty that the humblest-minded woman is persuaded that the man who may once have been in love with her can see her again with perfect tranquillity.

Vilpont had, truth to say, placed the very real preference he had felt for Pauline among other of his experiences of life. He had even, according to the wont of poets, embodied the episode of Vignes Ste. Marie in a Hermann and Dorothea idyl, which had a splendid success, and had been charmingly recited by Sarah Bernhardt.

Until the De Sayes had spoken to him of Madame Subar, Vilpont had not thought of her for years. This new play was undoubtedly founded on fact; but no recollections of Madame Rendu or her daughter had sharpened his pen.

As soon, however, as the once familiar name was pronounced, Pauline's image started from

8*

one of memory's cells. The pretty, girlish figure, with its coronet of bright hair, rose before him; the large eyes met his with a sweet welcome, while the lips kept their gravity. He closed his eyes for a second to banish the sight, and said in an irritable voice, "I detest all young married women."

"Very polite," said Stephanie, rising, and making him a coquettish curtsey.

"Oh! you are no longer in that category; but I should prefer visiting even you two or three years hence."

This novel profession of faith was due to a newly-developed jealousy—the lees of his former feeling. He did not call on Madame Subar.

They were, however, sure to meet—people always do who have any reason for desiring to keep asunder. There is a magnetism in this world which draws those together who are either to unite or to combat.

The meeting of these two took place at a ball during the Carnival. Pauline knew she had flushed as he came towards her. He approached with the nonchalant manner with which he had learned to veil all his emotions; that is, when he had any. Probably on this occasion he was not so unembarrassed as he appeared. He sat down by her, and began at once to speak of St. Gloi, inquiring after M. and Mme. Rendu, and for all those he chose to call his "old friends." What a misnomer!

What did he care for those people, or they for him?"

One exception, however, there was—he still retained a grateful recollection of old Madame Jorey. "She and I exchange letters at the New Year," he said. "She sends me *étrennes* of the produce of her farm, and I send her bonbons from Serandet."

Pauline thought of the Sunday bonbon-making, but to all appearances he had forgotten it.

Then he spoke of Stephanie. It was a pleasure, he said, to see how happy she and De Saye were. "She gave me quite a severe lecture on my ignorance and misrepresentation of marriages and the way they are made. By the bye, I understand you also were dreadfully shocked by my last play."

"'Shocked' is not the right word," replied Pauline, in a voice unfamiliar to him, it was so firm and grave. "I was disappointed. I had hoped for something better than a satire, almost a caricature."

"Spoken with the eloquence of party spirit. You are enrolled among matrons, and object to the divulging of the secrets of your class. I am a realist, and describe what I see. As you are aware, I live by my pen, and I should starve if I painted pastorals."

"But there is also a beautiful side of human nature to those who look for it. You will not deny there is beauty as well as ugliness in the world," said Pauline.

" But suppose I shame one mother, one only, from a dishonest bargain. have I done nothing against the ugliness and for the beauty of our many-sided nature ? "

" That is one way of viewing it, certainly, but—"

" You still remain my adversary." He stopped, and added, " Here, I believe, is M. Subar. Shall we take him as umpire ? "

Pauline introduced the two men to one another, and after a few conventional phrases, having no reference to the subject in dispute, M. Subar walked his wife off.

" Your friend, the author, looks just like any one else—not a bit like a hero of romance," said Léon, as they drove home.

" Why should he ? " asked Pauline, dryly. " Those sort of men usually affect something to make people stare ; but this play-writer has nothing of the Bohemian about him."

When Pauline was left to herself, she experienced that dissatisfaction we so often feel after an evening in company ; haunted by a wish we had not said, or looked, or done one particular thing, the something, in reality, having passed quite unobserved. She was displeased, disappointed, and would have been puzzled to explain why. Was it that the reality of the present had marred the ideal of ' the past ?

Vilpont had asked her which was her reception day. She hoped he would not come. She did not care to see him again ; and she was convinced, without needing to think twice about it, that he and Léon would not suit one another.

Vilpont, on his side, had intended to present himself immediately at the Subars, and then he had hesitated. There is no accounting for attraction or repulsion; and she who is no Circe for the many may be dangerous to one in particular. Years ago Vilpont had jokingly called Pauline "dangerous." His present hesitation was significant, but it did not last long.

He had not required to talk ten minutes with M. Subar to fathom his shallowness. "Poor thing! poor little Pauline! how she had boasted of having ideas and opinions of her own, and tied to such a donkey! Handsome, though, and rich; after all, many a charming woman has adored an ass."

Vilpont made his appearance in Madame Subar's drawing-room on her second reception-day, after he had met her at the ball.

# CHAPTER V.

### A FIRST WARNING.

SENTIMENTS and seeds have a decided analogy—a seed, hidden away for centuries, when brought to light, fructifies; a sentiment, forgotten for years, laid bare by some chance word or act, suddenly asserts its vitality, and grows apace. The little seed which had fallen into Pauline's young heart five years ago was germinating. It happened to her, as it has happened and will happen to so many, to be blind to the cause of the sudden gilding of her days —of what was transforming the dull to the bright.

The sharp Zelie was not slow to remark that at this time Madame Subar broke out frequently into song; shakes, *roulades*, loud and gleeful, often startled the ears of the *valetaille*. Joseph wagged his head slowly on one of these occasions, and sagely remarked that " nothing made women happy but balls and dress."

" *Vieille bête!* " ejaculated his wife, with a look that made Joseph say—

" What is it, then ? "

" Nothing that concerns thee," was the mysterious answer.

M. Vilpont had become a regular visitor at the Subars; so much so, that Léon one day startled his wife by saying, " I do wonder,

Pauline, you can bear so much talk about poetry and pictures."

"What else can I talk about, Léon ? I don't understand anything of horses and dogs."

" I suppose I know a good picture when I see it as well as any one else, though I can't speechify for an hour about how it is done."

" But you would care about finding out the painter's method if you were studying painting, as I am doing."

" You would do a great deal better if you rode out with me, instead of making yourself a mess with paints; and what's the use ? "

" Of no use, but a great pleasure to me ; and I wish I could ride, but I have no courage."

Such conversations were the mere passing clouds which threw momentary shadows across Pauline's sum of content.

There was small similarity between Pauline's and Vilpont's feelings. She was happy in her unconsciousness of danger. Had any one hinted to her that her feet were straying into perilous paths, she would have drawn her little figure up to its highest possibility, and scornfully smiled at the warning, if, indeed, she did not beg the adviser never again to cross her threshold.

But Vilpont had no such blindness. He was one of those men as far from being supremely good as he was from being supremely bad. He was, in fact, such as most men are—prone to slide into wrong-doing, but not deliberately to walk into evil ways; in short, a man of impulse, which is the same as saying he would never of *malice prepense* do a wicked deed.

It is difficult, no doubt, for a man who sees a charming woman's eyes brighten when he appears, to resist the temptation to see that effect pretty often. Vilpont had had more than his share of successes of that kind, but never with any one so unsophisticated and sincere as Pauline.

At first he studied this lighting up of her eyes, and the transformation of the whole face, growing so transparent that her very soul looked out at him, as men do who in the interest of their art are always on the alert for symptoms of the passions—a study seldom free from danger.

Now and then a qualm of conscience made Vilpont absent himself; but this half-sacrifice only resulted in giving a keener pleasure to both at their next meeting. Whether mortals have or have not guardian angels may be disputed; what is sure, is, that we, none of us, err without a warning, or indeed many warnings; and Pauline was to experience this.

It was in a call after one of these absences that Vilpont interrupted himself in an interesting account of the visit he had just made to the " Forges de Creuzot," to say suddenly, " Surely you are infested with rats and mice."

Pauline repeated in amazement, " Rats ?—mice ? "

" I assure you," he answered, " I am

tempted to strike as Hamlet did when he heard a noise behind the arras."

" I don't the least understand," said Pauline.

" Ah! you are not aware of my insane horror for such vermin. Allow me to look round. Do you not hear something—a horrid, stealthy step ?"

Pauline's change of color was sufficient answer. She did hear a slight sound, such as a velvet-footed cat might make stealing on its prey.

Vilpont went on—"I should advise you, Madame Subar, to be on your guard against letting such noisesome intruders gain a footing in your pretty hotel."

Pauline, who now understood that he suspected some one of trying to overhear their conversation, said as calmly as she could, " I will certainly have the matter looked into."

After an interruption of this nature, to resume their conversation was impossible ; the fine golden thread had been snapped past knotting together again.

There are many persons like Pauline, who live stone-blind to the suspicions they excite or the traps laid for them, until the moment when light, striking into the darkness, shows them, too late, their peril.

Happily, Madame Subar's attention was roused to what had hitherto passed unheeded —a strangeness lately in her maid's bearing and conversation, a levity of speech and an undue familiarity of manner, to which she began now to attach a meaning.

For instance, only a few days ago, Zelie, while dressing her hair, had spoken of having been to see M. Vilpont's new play, and had described with ecstasy the dresses of the actresses.

"Those are the happiest women in the world, madame—always applauded, and the finest, richest gentlemen at their feet. If I were to live my life over again, I would never marry; and you, madame—"

"I am sure you have nothing to complain of," Pauline had answered; "you have an excellent husband."

"I don't complain, madame; but after a year husbands look on their wives as nothing more than a bit of furniture—wives are no better than the men—fine ladies do safely what would ruin a waiting-maid's character."

Pauline had shown her displeasure by requiring some service which put an end to Zelie's observations.

All this flashed back upon her, together with Stephanie's warning, supported now by Vilpont.

No one seeing a lion in his path could have started back with a greater mingling of despair and terror than did poor Pauline at this discovery. The bitterest drop to swallow was that Vilpont should have divined that she was suspected by her own servant, and of what she was suspected. What had she ever done to deserve such an indignity? Her first feeling was anger against Vilpont; she would shut her door to him—do so openly; it would prove how perfectly indifferent she was to him. Had he possessed any delicacy, he would not have shown her so brutally the interpretation put on his visits.

O dear Heaven! her own familiar friend, and her own menial!

All the pride of woman's nature rose up in arms.

Why not have left her in ignorance? Was there anything to hide? The more she was watched, the better.

Pauline was like one, who, no believer in ghosts, yet wandering in the dark, is frighted by the shadow of a nameless horror.

She wanted advice—she yearned to confide in some one—but to whom? She dared not tell her mother. Beforehand, she knew how severe would be her mother's sentence—she had a prescience of all the cruel words she would launch at Vilpont; and Pauline, however she might blame his want of tact, exonerated him from any other fault. He had never spoken a word or looked a look that all the world might not have taken cognizance of. He had been very kind—the only one who ever led her thoughts to any higher subjects than scandal or the amusements of the gay world— the only one to whom she seemed always to have something to say. "Ah! what a blank in her life, if she had to give up his visits!"

# CHAPTER VI.

### ON THE QUI VIVE.

DINNER cannot be delayed because the lady of the house is a prey to painful misgivings. Pauline was a tyro in concealment, and she had thought so long how she should behave to Zelic, that she had let the dressing-hour pass unattended to.

Léon was silent during dinner—very unusual for him, who could only manage to think by the help of speech. He belonged to the pretty numerous class who talk in order to understand their own thoughts, the consequence rather of a want of early training, than of any original defect of intelligence.

At this day's dinner he let his words drop as though the fate of nations depended on them. Pauline labored, on her side, to keep up a conversation that should hide from the servants their master's ill-tempered taciturnity. But as soon as they were alone in the *salon*, she gave up the struggle, and took a book. Not that she cared to read, but that she wanted to reflect whether she should follow her inclination, and mention that she was no longer well pleased with Zelic. She hesitated, from an instinctive repugnance to mix up Vilpont's name in the discussion that must ensue. She foresaw that even should she avoid any men-

tion of him, Zelie would be less reticent, and
Pauline, with a thrill of terror, allowed to
herself that Zelie was sufficiently artful to
manage to change their relative positions from
that of accused to accuser. This hour was
perhaps as sad a one as Pauline would ever
experience in her life. It was then she
learned the lesson that in this world of ours
necessities will arise which force the most
candid soul to desire to throw a veil over the
truth.

While thus debating within herself, Léon
suddenly asked, "What is it that so absorbs
you, Pauline? One of Monsieur (with an
emphasis on the Monsieur) Vilpont's plays?"

"No, some stories by a new author."

"All on the same subject, no doubt—teaching women to care for any one but their own
husbands."

"Claude Blonet, my present hero, is an ap-
prentice in love with his master's daughter.
The style is charming."

"I did not know you were so learned as to
be able to play the critic of style ; probably
you have been taking lessons in the art."

"Criticism is easy, and art is difficult,"
quoted Pauline ; "but what is the matter,
Léon ?"

"Nothing is the matter. Except that it is
not very amusing to have a wife with her head
always buried in books. I did not bargain
for that, you know. By the way, why are you
not going to the opera this evening ?"

"It is not my night for the box, but we might go somewhere else."

"Thank you. I don't approve of taking you on chance to any theatre."

Pauline laid aside her book, and went to the piano. Just as she had begun to sing, Léon rang the bell furiously. "I want the brougham," he said to the servant, and left the room without a word to his wife.

How was it possible for her to imagine that Léon's ill-humor and his observations, so apt to the tenor of her thoughts, were merely a strange coincidence; that he had hit at random, and that his annoyance was caused by a wound to his vanity in which she had no share. Irritated as he was (and what an amount of menace, it had seemed to her, he had imparted to the Monsieur before Vilpont's name!) she trembled to think what might have been the consequences had she made her complaint of Zelie.

She was startled out of her uncomfortable reflections by the sound of the *timbre* announcing a visitor. It was the young Madame de B——, one of the most fashionable of the great ladies of Paris.

Pauline was surprised, for hitherto her acquaintance with Madame de B—— had been ceremonious and superficial.

There were assuredly no affinities between the two ladies—the one resembling a wild wood flower—the other, one of those multi-petalled, multi-shaded roses, the pride of modern horti-

culture. Madame de B—— was by turns
aristocratic, democratic, artistic, flying high,
stooping low, volatile as a child, restless as a
bird; she believed herself the sport of a warm
heart and ardent feelings, when her poor heart
was as innocent of her vagaries as any stone,
her head alone being in fault. "*Mauvaise
tête*," said her admirers. Her person, like her
character, was an assemblage of contradictions.
The upper part of the face handsome, almost
grave, the mouth and jaw heavy, and trench-
ing on the vulgar. In figure, she was what
Lord Byron stigmatized as " dumpy," but with
hands and feet ideally perfect.

Madame de B—— advanced to Pauline with
all the familiarity of intimacy. " I astonish
you, *ma belle*—your pretty blue eyes speak
clearly; you see before you a victim. My
aunt, on whom I reckoned for the opera this
evening, has played me false—got some kind
of fever. It's frightful; how easy it is for
people to go out of the world ! Well, *ma très-
belle*, as I was driving past, I saw lights in
your windows. Here is my salvation, I
thought—*crac*—and here I am ; you will be
amiable as you look, and come with me. M.
de B—— hates to see me in my box without
some other petticoat by my side—save me a
lecture."

" But I am not dressed," said Pauline.

" An affair of five minutes : some flowers in
your hair—a *burnous*—you don't need any
paint—what a happiness !—fleeting, like all

that is charming. There, I have rung for
your woman."

Pauline submitted; in fact, relieved to be
saved from a *tête-à-tête* with her thoughts.

As they entered the box Madame de B——
said, "There's your husband, I declare; and
he sees us."

Léon was in one of the orchestra-stalls, and
met Pauline's eyes with the most agreeable of
smiles.

"Monsieur Subar has a look of Monsieur
de B——," said the Countess, studying him
through her double opera-glass. "Both are
handsome enough, at least every one tells me
my husband is an Adonis. When he proposed
for me, you would have said the happiness of
my life was to be founded on his having a fine
nose. To tell you the truth, *ma très-chère*, I
have but a poor opinion of men. I don't consider them our equals, do you? How can I,
when I see what fools we can make of them;
I amuse myself with experimenting on their
facility for swallowing any bait?" Madame
de B—— was garrulous as a linnet; she
listened to herself with complacency, persuaded she was a wit. She only listened when
—— sung. "He is my present occupation,"
she said. "See how he looks this way;
amusing—he fancies I am in earnest. He is a
perfect ape—but I am tired to death of good-
looking men; are not you?"

The most reasonable conversation would
certainly not have calmed Pauline's nerves as

well as this senseless chatter. Taken together with the music and Léon's smiling aspect, she came to the conclusion that she had been making mountains of mole-hills. Her mind worked with that double power innate in us all, which allows of the flowing of two currents of thought as unmingled as the waters of the Arve and of Lake Leman.

Before she closed her eyes for the night, she had the satisfaction of thinking how sillily she had allowed imagination to alarm her. To this desirable end had contributed Léon's first words after their return home.

"I was so glad to see you with Madame de B——," said Léon. "She is in the best world of Paris; cultivate her acquaintance, and she will get every palace door opened to you. You should take some hints from her dress— you looked like a little nun by her side; out of justice to me, you should try to be more attractive." All this time Léon was studying himself in a large mirror.

The most modest woman in the world will resent her husband's depreciation of her appearance; so Pauline replied with a certain pique, "Her present caprice is an admiration for ugly men."

"Hm; words are used to conceal thoughts, my innocent one," retorted the self-satisfied husband.

Life for the Subars went on as before, until the end of the Carnival. Pauline then made known her intention of going into Retreat.

9

She had chosen the convent in which she had been educated, and where she would find Madame Agnes on leave of absence from England.

Léon, on being informed of his wife's project, laughed, and said, " What *mignons péchés* are you going to repent of?—but of course, I am not going to interfere. Few husbands would venture on doing so in such a case."

Vilpont sneered when he heard of the matter. " Droll! how you women love extremes— roses to-day, ashes to-morrow, anything for a sensation."

" And you men?" exclaimed Madame de B——, now as often to be met in Pauline's *salon* as Vilpont. " And you men—do you differ much from us? Pretty examples you set us, with your oscillations—now at the shrine of virtue, and piff-paff, bowing the knee to some ugly Delilah. You want all the fun for yourselves. Thank you, I like my share in the frolics."

" I have no objection," said Vilpont. " Thank Heaven I have no stakes to lose!"

How that " Thank Heaven!" pained Pauline. With a woman's sensitiveness she took it as a negation of the feeling she believed he had once cherished for her. Poor soul! pity to think how she grieved over those light words.

# CHAPTER VII.

## GOSSIP.

N'est plus amour qui bien aimer faisait.
Les faux amants l'ont jété hors de vie.
Amour vivant n'est plus que tromperie ;
 Pour franc amour, priez Dieu, s'il vous plait.

PAULINE remained in retreat during the whole of Lent. She resisted alike Madame Rendu's maternal warnings of the impropriety of such a protracted absence from her husband and Madame Agnes's admonitions as to her duty as a wife.

"I guess you have some sorrow weighing on you, Pauline ; nevertheless we must keep our lamps burning, and be found always ready at our appointed posts."

Pauline answered—"Do you remember my writing to you long ago—how long ago it seems —that I must expect trouble in my married life, having known none as a girl. The trouble has come, dear friend, and in a worse shape than any my ignorance of life at that time could picture. Ah ! dear madame, marriage in France has nothing in it of a Divine institution."

" A tragical-sounding phrase to express some annoyance," said Madame Agnes. " In real life, my dear child, we bruise our feet often

on the rough stones that lie on our path, but
they do not inflict incurable wounds. Ah!
you smile now, do you not, at what made you
shed tears as a child? So it will probably be
some years hence, nay one year hence, with the
trouble you feel so heavy now."

"The belief that some day the pain will
vanish does not cure the present smart."

"Ah, Pauline! the friction of life wears out
everything—joy, love, hope, sorrow, ambition,
all pass away, and—"

"Do not say any more, dear friend; if I believed you, I could not live."

"Poor child!—poor impatient child! who
will not let me remind her there is one
Staff on which she might lean and be sure it
would never break, let the burden of her sorrow be ever so great."

In some states of mind consolation chafes,
advice irritates; what the galled soul wants is
to be allowed to complain, to talk over its hurt
—in short, "to rail at Fortune in good terms
—in good, set terms."

Pauline turned with distaste from the wave-
less future to which Madame Agnes pointed,
and checked the outpouring of her heart.

The first face Pauline saw on her return
home was Zelie's unkind one. During Madame Subar's absence, Zelie had busily spread
her venom through all the neighboring *loges de
Concierges:* Monsieur Subar was madame's
victim—madame neglected him cruelly, caring
for nothing but her music and painting, al-

ways taken up with a queer set who wrote
plays and painted pictures, quite indifferent
whether monsieur liked such goings-on or
not.

" Dame ! " objected one of the gossips, " if
she does no worse, she is an angel. Look at
Mesdames A——, or B——, or C——. Mon
Dieu ! are they wild ? "

On which Zelie would raise her shoulders as
high as her ears, and say, " Still waters are
dangerous ! "

But Zelie's sharp wits speedily understood
that the chance of having any hold on her
mistress had disappeared. She ceased her familiarity, and waited on Madame Subar with
the haughty air of a captive Zenobia. Her
hatred of Pauline, however, was daily deep-
ened by the little stabs to her vanity which Léon
so often gave by laughing at the contrast between her dark skin and his wife's fairness.

His greeting to Pauline was in this wise—

" So you have flown back to the nest ! Why,
my kitten, you are as pale and thin as a saint
—isn't she, Zelie ? *Ma foi*, you two make a
capital contrast. I'll have you painted together." And then Léon rattled on. " You
know I have a horse to run on Sunday. Get
madame a brilliant toilette for the occasion,
Zelie—blue sets off her complexion, you know ;
and *apropos, ma chère*, your adorer, the play-
writer, has transferred his allegiance. *Les
absents ont toujours tort, ma chérie.* That
hits more than our ex-friend, eh ! However,

you are as pretty as a heart, so I forgive your desertion."

Léon could not help his shallowness; you might as well have been wroth with him because he had black and not gray eyes, and Pauline was decidedly wrong to resent his want of depth. His taste and his capabilities were those of a mirror, laying entirely among externals.

When M. Subar had taken his leave, Zelie remarked, "Monsieur did not perhaps like to tell madame, but all Paris is talking of madame's friends, M. Vilpont and the Countess de B——."

Zelie licked her lips with the relish of a fox who has just devoured a lamb.

Pauline said, "I never believe anything I hear and only half that I see, Zelie. There would be no living in peace with the people about one, if we trusted either our eyes or our ears."

Zelie was silenced as much by madame's look and tone as by the significant words.

The *chères mesdames* who filled Pauline's *salon* on the first day she received visits after her return, like Zelie, had nothing more at heart than to retail the last piece of scandal. The question, "Have you heard of poor Madame de B——?" was a real *bonne bouche.* "No retenue—no *savoir-vivre*—no respect on either side for *les convenances*," rattled like hail about Pauline's ears.

"*Ma foi*, ladies," said a gentleman, "do not

blame Vilpont too bitterly; women never believe in a man till they have forced him to
compromise them."

"Infamous!—horrible!—unjust!" . came
from all sides.

"Have you seen the arch-culprit, the *mau-
vais sujet?*" asked one lady of Madame Subar.

"No—but let us change the subject; either
he or Madame de B—— may come in at any
moment."

"She would not dare."

"Why not? scandal is not proof. If every
one were found guilty on the *on dits* of society,
which of us would escape."

Pauline had never read Shakespeare, but
noble hearts resemble one another in all ages
and nations.

"You are angelically charitable, my dear
lady," said the cynic, who had thrown the lar-
gest stone at Madame de B——.

Visitors stayed long, in the hope of seeing
Vilpont's meeting with Pauline; for in Paris,
perhaps also elsewhere, no possibility as to
"our neighbor's sentiments or deeds is left out
of the sphere of conjecture." Vilpont, preferring to meet Pauline when not alone, did
not disappoint the general expectation. He
could not hide from himself that the story she
must have heard would displease her, but he
had no conception of the stab it had given
her.

"After all, what is it to her?" he had said
to himself. "We are very good friends, but

that gives her no right to resent anything I please to do." Nevertheless, he could not get rid of an unwillingness to meet her eye. . Keen watchers saw his sallow face take on a purpleish shade as he went up to Madame Subar, but they detected no change of color on her face. He alone was aware of a momentary quiver of her upper lip.

As generally happens, the one subject to be avoided was always floating upwards. Pauline, alluding to her own absence, said that six weeks was sufficient to make one feel like arriving from the antipodes, quite behind-hand as to fashion and news.

Very significant smiles appeared on every countenance. "Ungrateful!" exclaimed the cynic. "Have all our pains to enlighten you been in vain?"

Pauline sought safety in speaking of the coming races and of her husband's horse.

"What is it called?"

"Escapade."

Another sitter gave meaning to the name.

Then some one asked Pauline if she had seen "*Frou-frou.*"

And another kind-hearted person inquired of Vilpont which he would recommend—"*Le Supplice d'une Femme,*" or "*Frou-frou?*"

Vilpont left off biting the ends of his mustache, and in his turn put a question—"Recommend! in what way?"

"Oh! to Madame Subar, as she has seen neither."

" Either or neither," he said, " they are both
clever and both painful; but Madame Subar
might look on at such tragedies as angels do
on the sins of mortals, with the pity innocence
gives to guilt."

" A pretty compliment ; but remember, monsieur, addressed as it is to one person, it makes
you a hundred enemies."

" Madame, the title of enemy from ruby lips
does not alarm me. I accept your challenge."

" Not at all, there is no challenge," replied
the lady, and not feeling at a safe distance
from this practised freeshooter, turned to
Madame Subar with a hasty, " Sans adieu, ma
belle."

Vilpont took his leave at the same time,
escorting his fair enemy to her carriage.

" The audacity of that man is beyond belief!" exclaimed another lady, once sure he
was out of hearing.

" As to that, this affair gives him another
feather in his cap," said the cynic.

" He had a full *panache* of such already,"
was the rejoinder.

What an underlying ferocity there is in
social intercourse! How cleverly, or rather
cunningly, little thrusts are given, little mortifications inflicted! How people feed their
darkness on others' sunshine! No one, who is
not blind, or deaf, or stupid, but must have
suffered from the irritation social contact gives.
How little of the probability of kindness we meet
with—nay, where it exists, is it not often mis-

9*

taken for weakness, want of talent? Sharp, biting remarks are repeated with admiration, but not the kind words with which we bridle the devil of unkindness which lurks in us all.

# CHAPTER VIII.

## MEASURING A LANCE WITH SOCIETY.

Laissez tranquille la fausse vindicte humaine, la conscience fait largement son ouvrage.

THERE are cheerful households under the sinister shadow of Vesuvius—people married and made merry until the Deluge overtook them; there was dancing before, during, and after the Reign of Terror; and even at the moment when the terrible shock of war was imminent in 1870, all the gay world of Paris was thinking of and preparing for the concert and ball to be given by a princess as her banquet and adieu to her acquaintance.

A good-natured, aristocratic member of the Jockey Club took compassion on Léon Subar, and made interest for an invitation for M. and Mme. Subar.

When Léon received the inestimable card, he actually put his heels together and jumped for joy. "Now I am happy," he exclaimed. Poor Pauline! he was her husband, and she was bound by oath to honor him. Well, she obeyed him as well as she could, devoting herself to milliner and dress-maker with much the same feeling she would have in dressing a doll to please some child.

The important evening arrived, and Léon

was graciously pleased to approve of his wife's
dress. " I wish you would, just for this once,
put a touch of rouge below your eyes; I want
my kitten to be noticed."

" In the first place, I have none," she said ;
" and as I am not accustomed to wear it, I
might rub it into streaks, like Madame D——,
you remember, and that would be worse than
pale cheeks."

" There's some sense in that; I must put up
with you as you are. Ah! by the bye, I have
taken on extra men for the evening: one for
your cloak, and one for mine ; at such places
there is always a call for ' *les gens de Monsieur
un tel*,' and only one footman appearing would
raise a laugh at our expense."

" I begin to think what is called the ' great
world ' a very paltry one," said Pauline.

" It's you who are a delightful little simple-
ton, my angel. Next year I mean that we
should be naturalized among the very highest
—my fortune is doubling. We will go to
Rome this winter ; that's the surest way, I am
told, of getting on with the Faubourg—and your
being a pious kitten will be a help."

Pauline was silent—she was bound by oath
to honor and obey him.

Though they reached the princess's hotel
early, the rooms were already well filled. As
Pauline glanced round she saw Madame de
B——, but Madame de B—— strangely isolated, a very decided space left on each side
of her. She was standing, while near her men

were seated; chivalry was clearly not in their
way, and probably her sharp tongue or her contempt for their attentions while she was a leader
of fashion, stirred them to take their revenge.

Madame de B—— was noted for her spirit,
but she was evidently now ill at ease; the most
courageous woman shrinks from being avoided
in a *salon*. As Pauline's eyes fell on her,
Madame de B—— turned to one of the gentlemen nearest to her and said something, probably made some sarcastic remark on his politeness, for he rose and left his chair vacant.
Madame de B——, after a minute's hesitation,
availed herself of the vacant seat; in five minutes she was again obviously left alone. Just
then the poor woman's eyes met those of Pauline with the dumb beseechingness of some
animal in pain. With her old impulsiveness,
Pauline yielded to the appeal, and crossing the
room, seated herself by the Pariah's side. As
she did so, she caught sight of Léon's flushed,
angry face.

The little scene had been marked by some
unnoticed spectators—by the noble hostess and
her nobler guests. As they passed round the
circle, the greatest lady of the group bent her
lovely head to Madame de B——, who was
known to her, while the hostess said in a loud,
clear voice to Pauline, as she offered her hand,
" Bien charmée de vous voir, chère madame,"
although she had not an idea who the *chère
madame* was; but she did know that her
pretty incognito had a brave, generous heart.

Wonderful how many persons recovered their eyesight, recognizing Madame de B——; but society, like all tyrants, is mean.

The next morning at breakfast, Léon said, with some asperity of tone, "Well, for a woman who is dead frightened for a horse, you are astonishing. I would rather have leaped twenty fences than have done what you did last evening. I declare my heart stopped beating when I saw you cross the room and sit down by that mad coquette. Once is enough; don't you attempt to play the Quixote for all the idiotic women in Paris. If you want to get on in the world, follow the world's opinion —at least, never go contrary to it. That's a maxim I got out of a book, so you will not dispute its sense. Scratch Madame de B——'s name off your list, if you are wise."

"Time enough next winter," said Pauline, wearily. "I want change of air, Léon. I am only a provincial, and Paris is too much for me; besides, every one is going."

"Where do you wish to go? It is too soon for Trouville or Baden-Baden."

"I should be so glad to go for a little to St. Gloi. Mamma presses so much for a visit from us."

Pauline understood the meaning of Léon's shrug of the shoulders, and added, "If you care to stop longer in Paris, I could go alone at first, and you might join me later."

"You are not such a loving wife as Madame de Saye; she will not let De Saye go a foot without her."

" And the Jockey Club and the races, etc., etc.," laughed Pauline.

" Oh! well, I do not complain; it's very natural a girl should wish to be with her mother, so that is settled. You will not want Zelie to go also, I suppose ? "

" No; I shall only take Marie—she belongs to St. Gloi."

" What a virtue ! " said Léon, satirically.

The following morning Pauline received a card before she had left her dressing-room.

" Bring Madame de B—— to me here, Zelie ; and then leave us."

As soon as they were alone, doors shut and *portières* drawn, Madame de B—— said, " I am afraid you would rather not have had my visit ; at least I argue so, from the frown Monsieur Subar gave me as I passed him on the stair—he who was ready a few days ago to fetch and carry at my bidding. That, however, does not matter. I have come to tell you that I shall never forget your kindness last evening, you dear, good woman. It is out of gratitude, and for nothing else, that I will say to you what ropes should not drag from me, that I am better than I seem. I have been imprudent, audaciously imprudent, because I knew I was clear of any real fault. I wanted to amuse myself—life is so horridly tame—and that man's nonchalance piqued me ; now you have the truth. I wonder why

women like me should be born?" Here
Madame de B—— wiped her eyes.

Pauline kissed her, not knowing what to
say after Léon's prohibition of the day before.

"Do you know what Monsieur de B——
said to me about this stupid gossip? Why,
that none but a *parvenue* would have got herself into such a silly scrape. It's true I have
only common puddle in my veins. Monsieur
le Comte wanted money for himself, and my
mother wanted rank for me, and so the bargain was made. However, he has behaved
very well on this occasion—we are going to
appear this summer in a new domestic character. Tell Monsieur Subar that Monsieur de
B—— does not approve of gentlemen treating his wife uncourteously; or rather, say
nothing about it—if the occasion offers, Monsieur Subar will find that out for himself.
Bah! what an ingrate I am, to be fuming and
fretting at a slight when I ought to be thank-
ing you on my knees for your kindness! I see
you do not know what to say to me, so I
will leave you. Shall it be *au revoir*, or
*adieu?*"

"I am going away to St. Gloi, to stay with
my father and mother for a little," returned
Pauline, evasively.

"Then adieu, my dear friend, for so I shall
always hold you. When I am at the pinnacle of
fashion next winter, I will patronize Monsieur
Subar for your sake. Adieu!" and gathering

up her dress, Madame de B—— ran lightly down the stairs.

"Poor thing!" thought Pauline. "I believe her heart is heavy for all that."

# CHAPTER IX.

## SPECULATIONS.

"One would think she wished to forget she was married," thought Madame Rendu when Pauline had been at home a few days.

The mother meditated gravely as she watched her daughter. Pauline had resumed all her former habits, as though the events of the last eighteen months had never happened. Her husband's name seldom passed her lips. They corresponded regularly; but unless questioned, she never mentioned him.

Madame de Saye, with her usual foolhardiness, spoke out what Madame Rendu thought. "I declare, Pauline, one would imagine you were trying to forget you were married! I shall write and advise Monsieur Subar to come and make himself remembered."

Pauline, in her gravest voice, said, "I advise you to let Léon and me decide for ourselves on what suits us best."

Naturally, being repressed in one quarter, Madame de Saye's loquacity rushed at full tide in every other.

But while St. Gloi was speculating whether Madame Subar was on the eve of a judicial or amicable separation, or her husband was entangled in speculations endangering his fort-

une, Pauline was regaining tranquillity of
mind. The bow had been strained to its utmost, and the moment had arrived when it
must break or be unbent. Her old home was
just what she required. After her experience
of Paris, she better understood that provincial
life which she had once found so cold. There,
attention is concentrated on what does not
change quickly; external things acquire a
sort of existence of their own, and become a
treasure-house for memory. The habits of
life which had once seemed so poor to her
were now a restorative and balm. They had
the charm of some old melody of restricted
compass—monotonous, but sweet.

What pleased her best, however, were her
walks, or those long hours on the lake with
old uncle Adhemar for her sole companion.
Neither felt any need of avowing their rever-
ential affection one for the·other. Pauline
understood now the old man's life, and he
guessed that she had measured a lance with
the difficulties of life, and had been sorely
wounded. He never questioned her, but let
her have the solace of repose. Uncle Adhemar knew that there are thoughts not to be
clothed in words—phantom thoughts, that pass
and cannot be seized; he knew that these
dreamy, vague reveries were in themselves a
refuge for a weary spirit. But Madame Jorey was ignorant of these delicate shades of
sympathy. She put the most indiscreet questions with her usual frankness. She wanted

to know the particulars of the last scandal about Vilpont, an outline of which had travelled to her through Madame de Saye.

"Is the woman very pretty?—did she care for him?—did he love her?" questioned the old god-mother, who dearly loved a romance.

"Madame de B—— is handsome; but as to their feelings for one another, I cannot say. From a few words Madame de B—— let fall, I believe there was very little foundation for all the evil gossip."

"Then I give him up," said Madame Jorey, with decision.

"Because he was silly, and not wicked?" asked Pauline, with a smile.

"Go along, child? what do you know of such matters?"

A month of quiet had gone quickly by, when Madame Rendu told Pauline that if Léon had no intention of coming at once to St. Gloi, she must go back to him.

"It was quite understood between us that he would join me as soon as he could," said Pauline.

"Well, write and say he must tell you his plans; the whole town is speculating about you. The Curé has told me, that though some say you have quarrelled with your husband, many more assert that he ordered *you* to leave Paris."

"Why need we mind such nonsense?" said Pauline.

"If you do not care about it, I do, Pauline.

Such nonsense, as you call it, never attached itself to me. You don't know the world as I do; and besides that, you break the force of habit, the strongest of all ties, and teach your husband he can do without you."

"I will write, mamma," and so Pauline did. Léon replied, that with each passing hour rumors of war were becoming louder and more generally believed, and rendered his remaining in Paris absolutely necessary.

Madame Rendu looked very grave as she read this letter. "Can you guess what he means?"

"Not in the least. Léon never talks to me of his affairs."

"That is very wrong, and must be your fault. A wife ought to be like the drag on a wheel, and keep her husband from running down-hill."

"Had I asked Léon any questions about money-matters, he would have pinched my cheek, and called me a wise kitten or a silly kitten."

"And whose fault is it if he looks on you in such a light? Do you think your father ever thought of speaking or thinking of me as a kitten?"

Pauline very nearly laughed, it seemed so utterly impossible that her father should have had sufficient courage to venture on such a liberty.

Madame Rendu continued—"Don't rest

satisfied with being a harmless wife; show you have some common-sense, and be useful."

"You cannot believe, mamma, how different the life we lead is to yours. Very often I only see Léon at dinner."

"I am sorry to hear it. Look at the De Sayes, always together. I am sure he never dreams of doing anything without consulting Stephanie, and she refers all her difficulties to her mother."

"But you see, mamma, Léon is Léon, and I am not Stephanie; I have no turn for her sort of management. And then the De Sayes live in the country, and we in Paris. Above all, I will not worry Monsieur Subar."

Madame Rendu sighed; she had far too much perspicacity to waste words, but she sent Pauline back to her husband under the escort of M. Rendu, who was privately ordered to find out the real cause which kept M. Subar in Paris.

It was M. Rendu's first visit to his son-in-law's house, and he was surprised and dazzled by the luxury of its appointments. At the end of a couple of days he wrote to Madame Rendu that he could perceive no cause for uneasiness. Léon had, he assured her, all the good spirits which belong to prosperous men. Léon had a talent which is not solely the appanage of the clever—where the motive was personal, he could keep his own counsel.

Madame Rendu replied in so many words, that monsieur had better remain in his pleasant quarters some days longer. She was in the midst of her *léssive* (a portentous wash), and could spare him with pleasure, and also with advantage to himself.

Will any one who was in Paris on the 16th July, 1870, ever forget that day?

Léon came in for the mid-day breakfast radiant. He was a handsome—nay, a very handsome man; and now, with his features lighted up with joy of a peril escaped, he might have stood as a model for the God of Day.

"Peace!" he exclaimed, "peace! and there is my thank-offering," and he threw a purse into Pauline's lap. Now, my kitten, go to Worth and get any number of costumes, and we will take wing for Trouville. Such a relief!" he added, addressing his father-in-law.

M. Rendu was startled by the intense expression Léon gave to the words; he understood, then, that some peril had been escaped.

Pauline said laughingly, "I never believe in evil till it comes."

"A fine politician you would make; and they talk of making women equal with men! *Trinquons*," and Leon clinked his glass against M. Rendu's.

"Take my advice, Léon," said M. Rendu, "and free yourself from all risks while it is yet time. Whatever danger you have run may reappear to-morrow, considering the situation of those who rule us,"

"Yes, yes," replied Léon impatiently; "trust me, I know what I am about."

M. Rendu wrote an account of this little episode to his wife, and then went out with his daughter for a drive, intending to return to St. Gloi the next day.

The evening papers shot a thunderbolt into every household in Paris. "War!" shouted Gramont. "The majesty of France has been insulted—war!"

At first Léon refused to believe his paper. He went out to seek for intelligence, and returned like a maniac; he stormed, raved, swore, tore his hair—wept. When Pauline made an attempt to obtain some explanation, this hitherto easy-tempered husband turned so fiercely on her that M. Rendu placed himself before his daughter.

With a wild oath the furious young man strode out of the room, banging the door with a force that shook the house. Never had Pauline witnessed before a scene of violence. She sat silent, pressing her hand on her heart to still its beating; her father, scarcely less agitated, stood by her stroking her hair.

"What can it be, papa?" she whispered.

"I am afraid he has lost money."

"Only that?"

"He may be ruined, my poor child."

"Oh! ruined, papa, that's a very big word. He may have lost something; but, you know, he is very rich."

"We must try to hope the best, my dear.

Thank God your old father will always be able to save you from poverty."

"But what would mamma say, and after all her trouble to get me a rich husband," said Pauline, with a bitter recollection.

"Hush! your mother did as she always does—for the best.. No one can see into the future—we walk blindly towards our fate. We are grieving now for one thing, and who knows, Pauline, what other sorrow is at hand."

"I am not really grieving, papa; at least, not about the money. Léon frightened me, and I am sorry for him. I know, papa, that money is a good thing, but not the best of all things. You and I are philosophers, papa; you used to say so—do you remember?"

Yes, he remembered, and more than Pauline dreamed of. They sat hand in hand for some time; at last she said, "Had I not better go and see after Léon?" Nothing proved clearer to M. Rendu how little husband and wife were to each other than this question. In any trouble *his* wife would have been by his side, a support on which he could lean—somewhat hard and rugged externally, but sound at the core.

"Certainly, my dear. Perhaps I had better go with you."

"No, papa; I am not afraid now. Poor Léon!"

She came back almost directly—"Léon is gone out, Joseph says."

"Oh! then all we can do is to wait."

10

Waiting was easy to the old man; he had practised patience for many a year; but Pauline, for all her boast as to her philosophy, could not follow her father's example.

"I should not mind what it was so that I only knew. It's the unknown that frightens me, just as I am frightened to be left in the dark."

M. Rendu had recourse to the newspaper, but she interrupted him very soon.

"Papa, you must have seen many things in your life; did you ever meet any one happy from beginning to end?"

"Yes, my dear; I believe I have been always happy."

To M. Rendu's surprise Pauline threw her arms round his neck, exclaiming, "Papa, you are an angel!" and burst into tears.

"It will do you good to cry, my poor little girl."

"O papa, papa! what a blessing to have a father like you!"

Pauline was right; the heart of a good father is one of nature's *chef-d'œuvres*.

Hours went by, and still Léon did not return. It must have been past midnight when Zelie came into the *salon* with a letter.

"When did it come?—who brought it?" asked Pauline.

"Monsieur left it with me, with orders not to give it to madame before this hour," answered Zelie, with even a greater assumption of her captive princess manner.

"Thank you, I shall not require you to-night."

Zelie flounced away with suppressed dignity.

Pauline's fingers trembled as she opened the envelope. She first read the enclosure to herself, and then handed it in silence to her father. The note ran thus :—

"CHÉRIE—It is a cruel necessity which obliges me to set off without an hour's delay for Marseilles; I hope to catch the next steamer for Algiers. I think it better to avoid seeing you, to escape the explanations which your father might believe himself entitled to ask. Besides, I shrink from your tears, and for these reasons I deny myself the happiness of embracing my pretty kitten. You will remain where you are till my return, which will be as soon as practicable. You had better get rid of one of the coachmen, and have all but your own horses sold. Joseph will see to that. You must not wear a melancholy face, and do not shut yourself up; receive every one as usual, and let yourself be seen driving in the Bois. In a month, or six weeks at longest, I shall be home again, in time for a trip in the autumn to Berlin.

"Be under no alarm, it will be easy to remedy my present mishap. I shall not write again before reaching Algiers. Zelie has her orders when to deliver this; you can trust her in everything. *Au revoir*, my adored angel. I embrace you as I love you.      LÉON."

"Well then, my dear, I suppose the wisest thing we can do is to go to bed."

"Good-night, papa—dear papa!" was all Pauline said; she made no comments on the letter, nor did her father.

Pauline had a keen sense of justice, and she was asking herself, "Did I deserve better from him?"

# CHAPTER X.

## PLAYED—AND LOST.

PAULINE was young, indifferent about money, because ignorant of its value; and being relieved of any fear as to Léon's safety, with the added comfort of her father under her roof, she slept a sound, refreshing sleep.

M. Rendu not being young, nor ignorant of the value of money, did not rest so well. From the manner of his son-in-law's departure, he argued the existence of some serious and pressing necessity, probably some involvement through one of the mad speculations of the day. The poor father lay awake composing a letter which he hoped would bring his wife at once to Paris. For him Pauline was still a child, and to leave her alone in that large house, with only the protection of servants, seemed impossible. His letter was written and sent off before he met Pauline at breakfast.

"It is a pity," he said, "that Léon has desired you to remain here; you would have been far safer with us at St. Gloi."

"Much happier, at any rate, papa. As to safety, I don't think Zelie, with all her ill-will, would quite run the risk of poisoning me."

"Ill-will? what makes you think she has any ill-will towards you?"

"It's no fancy, papa; she dislikes me be-

cause I am Léon's wife. She makes me understand in all sorts of ways that she does not consider me good enough for him; and perhaps
she is right."

M. Rendu said nothing in reply, but Pauline's words impressed him with a very vivid
desire that she should not be left to Madame
Zelie's guardianship.

"I have written to your mother, and I hope
she will come; she always sees what is best to
be done."

"I wish you could both stay with me till
Léon returns."

"Perhaps we may—that is what I should
propose. And now, Pauline, you must think
of arranging your household affairs. What
money have you?"

"Zelie manages the house and pays the bills,
papa; you must ask her."

But M. Rendu had no fancy for a conference
with the Algerine. "I had perhaps better
wait till your mother comes."

Madame Rendu came by the first train after
receiving his letter. She was even more
troubled than M. Rendu by Léon's mysterious
night, and still more exasperated by his desiring Pauline to remain in Paris, and by the
prominence given to Zelie.

"All your fault, Pauline; I told you what
would be the consequence of your making
yourself of no use."

"I might have been more active in housekeeping, mamma; but as Léon never spoke to

me of his affairs, how could I know anything about them ? "

" Well, well, when he returns, turn over a new leaf ; it's your duty to prevent his having any other confidante than yourself. That yellow vixen, I'll be bound, knows all about this matter and everything else."

" Take care, mamma," whispered Pauline, her eyes glancing round at the numerous doors, the convenience sometimes, but also the plague, of French houses.

" It's abominable," said Madame Rendu ; " she shall not stay."

" We must wait till Léon returns," was again whispered ; " and pray, don't offend her just now, mamma."

" What a silly woman you have been ! " was the rejoinder. " Who would ever have supposed Stephanie Jorey had double your sense ? "

It seemed to Pauline that every one united in holding up Stephanie as a model wife to her. It was rather hard to bear, after being accustomed for years to hear Stephanie spoken of as half a fool.

Léon's orders about the sale of his horses were carried into effect without Madame Su-bar being informed ; indeed, Zelie made it patent that she considered herself left in authority even over her mistress.

Poor Pauline so dreaded her mother's reproaches, that she strove to conceal that she was a mere cipher—that she reigned perhaps,

but assuredly did not govern. This did not
suit Zelie, very few persons had ever made
this half-African woman feel herself mastered; but in Madame Rendu she was aware
she had met her match, and Madame Rendu
she resolved to get rid of. This was difficult,
for Madame Rendu was blind to all imperti-
nence, and deaf to the most transparent hints.
But if the lady's patience was inexhaustible,
not so that of the housekeeper. Driven to extremity, Zelie at last told Madame Rendu, in
set terms, that M. Subar had not taken into
account any increase in his household expen-
diture!

"If you are in want of money, apply to
your mistress—the house expenses are no business of mine," said Madame Rendu, and
walked out of the room to prevent any retort.

"Who would have dreamed of a child of
mine being in such a situation?" mused Madame Rendu. "And yet I did my best; but
no, she would not be satisfied with any of
those we knew thoroughly, she must have
some one out of the common; and I vow to
Heaven I don't believe she cares a straw for
Léon. And he—well—he shall at least be
forced to get rid of the demon he has placed
over my poor, silly girl."

Perhaps at this time it dawned on the
mother that a girl's feelings merit some attention; for after this skirmish with Zelie she
said to M. Rendu, "One does for the best, and
it turns out for the worst," and then she told

him of Zelie's insolent behavior. They decided at once that Pauline must be supplied with money, and with such precautions as should save her from being pillaged by the housekeeper.

A week, and then ten days passed, and no news from Léon ; but though Pauline wondered every morning that there was no letter, she was clearly not at all uneasy.

"What's the use of anticipating disasters, mamma? no one is ever out of danger. The horses may run away with us to-day, and break our arms or necks. Time enough to grieve when grief comes."

This period was full of trial to Madame Rendu : for alas ! she could not rid herself of the consequences of her own act—who can ? No use to repeat that she had done for the best ; there was a barbed arrow in her breast. What might not arise from this marriage without love ?

However, all private vexations were for the time being thrown into shade by public events. Pauline's patriotic ardor had no bounds. Every other occupation was laid aside for the reading of newspapers. From morning till night she was engrossed by their contents. She was wild with joy at the success of Saarbrücken. "I knew we could not be defeated," she said, tears rolling over her pale cheeks.

She was not alone in her joy and faith that France was but beginning a series of victories. Every one knows the incredible, the sad story

10*

which made all Europe quake. Still the cry
went up to heaven that not a German should
ever recross the frontier.

There certainly exists among mankind beings who answer to henbane and nightshade
in the vegetable world. Zelie was one of
these abnormal creatures; she distilled venom
from the virtues that brought healthy influences to others. It was curious to watch how
this human belladonna tortured Pauline, with
venomous subtlety gathering and retailing
every sinister rumor. It was Zelie who
brought the first news of the defeats at Wörth,
Froschweiler, and Gravelotte, and that St.
Gloi was occupied by Bavarian troops. At
first the Rendus and Pauline treated this last
bit of information as one of Zelie's inventions,
for they now all understood her politics.

"It is a *ruse* to get rid of us," said Madame
Rendu; but a few hours proved that it was a
fact, a sad fact.

M. Rendu at once declared the necessity of
his returning to look after his house and property. St. Gloi being an open town, of course
no resistance could be offered; but men and
officers would be billeted on the inhabitants, re-
quisitions of money and provisions enforced.

"Stay here, papa," implored Pauline.
"What does the house matter?—if they burn
it down, we can get another; but if they kill
you, where shall I find another father?"

She wrung her hands in vain.

"I must go, my child; you do not understand how vital it is for all of us that I should neglect no precautions for the safety of our property."

M. Rendu believed with too much reason that his daughter's future comfort depended on the fortune he still retained.

Madame Rendu wavered a short while whether to go with her husband or stay with her daughter. "But Pauline is safe in Paris," she said, "and my place is by my husband's side in moments of trial."

Up to this moment Madame Rendu had looked on herself as a martyr to duty. She had outwardly made a show of respect to M. Rendu as head of the family, but inwardly she had held him unworthy of a superior woman such as she was. All at once she discovered, with a curious sort of alarm, that long years of life in common had woven a chain as strong as death, and that without the husband she had mentally despised life would have no meaning for her. Another of the examples of how many things in the world and in ourselves are only known by the results.

Pauline accompanied her parents to the station. They wished to go at once into the waiting-room, but she begged hard for another five minutes—those last five minutes passed in watching the hands of the clock that warns friends of the moment to say farewell. The trio were pacing up and down the platform, feeling too deeply for speech, when all of a sudden they found themselves in the midst of a crowd of drunken, noisy, excited soldiers, fugitives from some battle, ignorant of the whereabouts of their regiments, clamorous, ready for any deed, good or bad.

" *Entrez, entrez donc*, monsieur and mesdames," cried the guardian of the waiting-room ; " you have only just time."

" Come with us, Pauline," cried her mother.

Pauline, her heart fluttering with terror, was following her mother when the same guardian put her back with a surly—" But your ticket." No, she was not allowed to pass ; and as for her venturing back to get one, there could be no question of it—the half-mad soldiers were besieging the office.

The good-natured woman of the book-stall here interfered, and said she would take care of the young lady, and with this crumb of comfort parents and child bid one another farewell.

Piloted by her self-constituted protectress, Pauline reached her carriage unmolested ; but she was to witness more proofs of defeat before she reached home. On one of the *Places* on her road there was a great gathering of people, listening with marks of sympathy to the story of some other fugitives from the army. This time the men were dismounted dragoons, their gay uniforms torn and soiled —one his head bandaged with a bloody rag, another his arm in a sling made of a horse's girth—and so on, all in sorry plight. A collection was being spontaneously made for them, when some one cried out, " Who knows whether they are not Prussian spies ? "

The supposition was eminently absurd, but at such moments it is always touch and go with the reason of a crowd. A moment's pause, and then the bewildered fugitives, hustled, kicked, knocked down, were finally hauled along to the nearest guard-house.

As Pauline sat lonely in her large *salon*, her feelings were near akin to those of one shipwrecked on some desert island ; she might consider herself, with a color of reason, deserted by father, mother, and husband. It was very quiet—no noise in the streets, within not a sound, not even any of those daily necessities of social life which interrupt or prevent any lengthened meditation or self-communion. In these solitary hours by-gone hopes flashed past. She said good-by to them with the loving regret we give to dead friends. " I have played and lost the great stake of a woman's life," she said—" that is over. The future, what does it hold in reserve for me ? But after all, why speculate about it ? Time goes on his way and settles everything.''

Neither that day nor the next did Pauline see any one. Those of her acquaintances who had not already left Paris were probably either packing up their valuables, or sitting through weary hours at the Prefecture de Police, waiting for their passports to be signed. She had given up her drives. The fright experienced

on the day of M. and Mme. Rendu's departure
was yet too recent for further venturing forth.
"I walk in the garden at the back of the house,
going round and round like a squirrel in a
cage," she wrote to her mother.

No letter from Léon by the mail; probably,
then, he would arrive in person.

It was on the first of September, the day of
the fatal march to Sedan. France was breathless with expectation of a crowning victory, and
Pauline gave few thoughts, it must be confessed, to Léon. She was sitting almost buried
in newspapers, when she was startled by the
now unaccustomed sound of the visitor's *timbre*,
followed by the appearance of an old acquaintance. M. Belairs was the son of the principal
banker of St. Gloi, one of the many suitors she
had refused. She had never seen him since her
marriage, and his visit alarmed her. With
lightning speed her imagination conjured up
some misfortune to her parents. But M.
Belairs had nothing of the appearance of a
messenger of evil. He was rosy, fat, and
smiling—just what we usually call "the picture of happiness."

M. Belairs, on his side, thought Pauline the
very personification of prosperity, sitting charmingly dressed in the richly-furnished *salon* of a
fine hotel, between court and garden. It struck
him that she was prettier than formerly, and
he was laboring with a compliment that should
express this opinion, when the timbre sounded
again.

"It must be Monsieur Subar!" exclaimed Pauline, starting to her feet.

"Monsieur le Marquis de Kergeac," announced Joseph, and Vilpont followed the announcement. He was in deep mourning for his uncle, looking thin and dejected, a complete contrast to the sunny-faced banker's son.

"Monsieur Belairs is from St. Gloi," said Pauline, "and brings me excellent news."

"*Mais oui, monsieur,*" and off went Monsieur Belairs, repeating what he had just told Pauline.

Vilpont (as he shall still be called,) drew his chair back out of M. Belairs' sight, and shook his head as if in warning, but contradicted nothing. Pauline understood that Vilpont had also come on some mission. He sat silent, biting the ends of his mustache, as was his habit when annoyed.

At last Monsieur Belairs remembered he had no more time to spare, as he was to return to St. Gloi by the afternoon train.

He was no sooner out of hearing than Vilpont said, "The sooner you quit Paris the better—this evening rather than to-morrow morning—all that idiot said is mere nonsense; the most alarming rumors are current, and I assure you it is no longer safe for you to remain here."

"But your rumors may have no more truth in them than those of poor Monsieur Belairs," said Pauline. "Besides, I am hourly expecting Monsieur Subar's arrival; and he bid

me in his last letter on no account to leave
Paris."

"At that time he could never have dreamed
of the march of the Prussians on Paris."

Pauline actually laughed. "I almost wish
they would come, it might be as good a way of
getting rid of them as any other."

"My dear Madame Subar, even if we should
defeat them, Paris fighting can be no fit place
for you."

"I am not afraid," said Pauline. "I shall
stay, Monsieur Vilpont. Though I am only a
woman, I can do something for my country.
I can help the wounded; besides, why should I
place more reliance on what you say than on
Monsieur Belairs' news? He comes from the
very neighborhood of the war."

"Because Monsieur Belairs belongs to the
very large class of persons who think they get
rid of an evil by ignoring its existence."

Pauline had addressed him in a cool tone
bordering on contempt, and an entire want of
friendliness in her manner. He was at a loss
to understand this, having entirely forgotten
the unlucky scandal about Madame de B——.
He rose to take his leave, and advanced towards her with an outheld hand. She made
as though she did not perceive the gesture, and
with a slight bow, said, "Adieu, monsieur."

Vilpont had reached the door when, moved
by a sudden impulse, he turned back and said,
"How have I had the misfortune to offend you,
Madame Subar?"

" Pardon me, I am not offended—how could I be ?" she asked, with what she intended for a smile, but which was instead a sarcastic curl of her lip.

" That is not sincere—not like yourself," he rejoined, his eyes fixed on hers. Pauline was yet to Vilpont the only woman he would have wished for his wife. He had retained a tender interest in her, and, contradictory as it might seem on the surface, he had let himself drift into troubled waters with Madame de B—— to keep Pauline out of the chances of temptation. A deed, to be good, however, must be innocent; but in judging Vilpont we must remember that no one escapes the influence of the atmosphere in which he lives, and he had breathed long and constantly the perfume of the Flowers of Evil.

With the same old impetuosity which Madame Rendu used to call insufferable, Pauline flashed out, " No, I am not sincere in saying I am not offended. I think you behaved atrociously to Madame de B——."

Vilpont exclaimed, " Madame de B——! *Chère dame*, you are all wrong; you are accusing the lamb of devouring the wolf."

" I do not wish to hear anything on the subject. You asked me to be sincere, and I have answered you. Nothing you could say would change my opinion. I am sorry because we can no longer be friends."

" But I cannot submit to that award. I am no worse than any of the other men you receive; no worse, I am sure, than that fat acquaintance of yours, who has so successfully impressed you; you really have no right to banish me more than all the rest."

Pauline turned on him, " How have you the courage to address me in this way?—Adieu, M. Vilpont."

They had both been standing during this dialogue; Vilpont hesitated a moment after receiving this dismissal, then he stooped down, kissed the hem of her dress, and said, " This may be the last time we ever meet, and I will not go without telling you how sincerely I admire and revere you. Ah! Pauline, I lost my chance of happiness when I lost you."

He was gone without waiting for another word from her.

Pauline stood as he had left her, almost as stiff and cold as though she had been turned to stone. It might have been hours, it might have been minutes, for any count she had taken of time, when Zelie's entrance roused her. Then she turned away, and flung herself face downwards on the nearest sofa.

" Madame is ill?" asked Zelie in an unfriendly voice.

" Not ill, but frightened. I don't know what I ought to do. The Prussians are advancing on Paris."

" Madame must be Prussian in heart to believe that," retorted Zelie insolently.

" Are you out of your senses that you speak to me in such a tone?" asked Pauline, sitting up and facing her adversary, her inward pain showing itself in the shape of anger.

Zelic, as she herself expressed it, fell from the clouds. Madame had become a *mouton enragé*. But Zelic recovered something of decent politeness; she was no exception to the rule that the overbearing, insult where they dare, and draw in their horns where they dare not, butt. It was another woman in difficulty and anger who remarked, "that little spirits always accommodate themselves to the temper of those they would work upon—will fawn upon the sturdy-tempered person, and will insult the meek." *

Pauline's outburst of anger had not soothed her own feelings. Who ever wounded another without feeling a counterblow? She could not endure her solitude; she wanted to get rid of all self-communing; she had that desire of movement which seizes on us after any great mental emotion. She would go out, and try to see if there were any signs of alarm in the streets. She found all the great thoroughfares, such as the Champs Élysées and the Boulevards unusually quiet, and returned home, fatigued in body but reassured in mind. There is a great analogy between nature and war: hurricanes in the one, and violent convulsions in the other, are preceded by calms.

The next morning Zelic burst into her mistress's room, crying out:

* Richardson's *Clarissa*.

"Madame, what is to be done? What is to become of us? We are defeated; the Emperor "—here a gross gesture of contempt—"has given himself up to that monster, William; the Prussians are close to Paris."

"Impossible!" Pauline exclaimed, as so many have done and will do, when told of some unexpected, overpowering misfortune.

"But, madame, it is true. There is a Revolution; what are we to do?"

A general frenzy reigned in Paris. But clever pens have sufficiently described this period—a period which was fruitful of every phase of human credulity—of heroism, of imbecility, of contempt for facts; of every extreme of good and bad.

# CHAPTER XI.

## BON SECOURS.

No time now for vain regrets, for dreams, for introspection. It was a moment which taxed every one's judgment.

Twenty-four hours had made it too late for Pauline to go to St. Gloi. The railway was entirely given up to troops, and, in addition, the German army was also approaching by that very route. The road to England was still open, but she had all a Frenchwoman's horror of placing the sea between her and France. The few persons of her acquaintance still in Paris advised her to do as they were doing and cross the channel; while her trades-people assured her she was as safe in her hotel as she could be anywhere. A siege! They laughed the idea to scorn. Want of provisions, maddest of all suppositions.

Pauline wished to remain, and she found, as every one does, reasons in plenty by which to bolster up her wish. Though masters had fled, *concierges* remained; then why should she be afraid to do the same? A *concierge* was as easily killed as a duke, and having also but one life, would be as chary of that life as his Grace. Her own servants when questioned declared they had no fear, and would willingly stay and run whatever risk there might be.

Of course when they said so, they did not believe in the likelihood of serious privation or danger.

At this moment Zelie was in her best humor. She had gained experience of war in Algeria, and she set about at once laying in large stores of provisions that would keep. She obtained credit easily, for neither she nor her mistress would have had the means to pay for all that was stored in every closet of the hotel. Nor did she neglect to fill wood and coal cellars. Of wine there was already a plentiful supply.

A day later an evening paper mentioned the arrival of a mail from Algiers. It brought a few hurried lines from M. Subar. He hoped to start by the steamer in the ensuing week. He was well. Pauline was to keep up her spirits. He had managed to settle his affairs tolerably to his satisfaction. He concluded with a stupid imprecation on Germany, and a "*Je vous embrasse.*"

Pauline smiled as she refolded the letter, one of those smiles that are as sad as tears, and then sent for Zelie to bid her prepare for M. Subar's return.

Nearer and nearer came the Germans, and still all Paris ridiculed the idea of a siege. Communication by post with all parts of the country was open, and as long as people received and could send letters—as long as they could go in and out of the gates—no one believed it could be ever otherwise. The prov-

inces breathed nothing but war to the knife,
and were as incredulous as the Parisians as to
the possibility of a siege *en règle.*

Monsieur and Madame Rendu wrote daily,
requiring equal diligence from Pauline. They
were stricken with the universal blindness.
" Send your diamonds to the bank," advised
Madame Rendu. " It is just the moment
for thieves to congregate in Paris." Of actual
starvation, of bombs, of death from cold, none
even of the most determined prophesiers of
evil ever thought.

Zelie dissuaded her mistress from at once
taking her mother's advice. It would be
better to wait till M. Subar arrived. Whether
Zelie had any formed design or not when she
thus spoke, must remain for ever unknown.
Opportunity often makes the crime. But it is
safe to believe that neither good nor bad qual-
ities reveal themselves, without having in some
way previously betrayed their existence.
Characters do not change by sudden explo-
sions.

Madame de Saye would have been on her
guard, because Madame de Saye had all the
suspiciousness which belongs to a narrow
mind, and which acquired for her the reputation of good sense. She trusted no one further
than she could see with her own eyes. She
was fond " of wandering from house to house,
a tattler and a busybody, speaking things she
ought not," in one word commonplace, and
consequently popular. Whereas Pauline had

in her the spirit of a reformer, was opposed to existing usages and gave offence, such opposition being regarded as a mark of contempt, an assumption of superiority. She had, besides, conscientiousness in excess, and because she disliked Zelie, was on her guard lest such dislike should betray her into an injustice. Zelie was clever enough to understand this delicacy of her mistress's conscience, and mean enough to take advantage of it. So the diamonds remained where they were.

Nearer and nearer came the Germans, and still Paris scoffed at the probability of a siege.

Another ten days went by and brought not a line from Léon to account for his absence. Pauline, just as she would have done had the same thing occurred to an acquaintance, found excuses and framed explanations for this curious conduct.

"Madame's feelings for Monsieur will never turn her hair gray," remarked Zelie.

Pauline, in fact, was not herself aware that her equanimity under the circumstances was extraordinary. She suffered from none of those thrills and presentiments, shadows always in attendance on every strong affection.

In the meantime, what had seemed more unlikely to happen than that the tower of Babel should reach heaven became an undeniable fact. Paris was hemmed in by a circle of iron. No more letters from without. Those who were within were cut off from the rest of the world. Still every one said and every one believed that this state of things could not last. There was excitement, agitation, but no discouragement. Not one soul ever contemplated the possibility of a capitulation. In the city was abundance of provisions, sufficient for the necessities of months. There was an army within the gates sufficient for defence. MacMahon and Bazaine would come to the rescue. The Germans would find themselves in a trap. Bazaine was then the man of the hour. Trochu, a demi-god. Times change.

A cursory observer would have discovered nothing unusual in the streets during the day; it was only at night that Paris looked unlike itself. By ten o'clock all the cafés were closed, the Boulevard silent and deserted.

Naturally all the usual pleasures or occupations of life, to speak only of private life, had become impossible. Men congregated to discuss events or probabilities. Women either passed their days in running after news, or, like Pauline, obeyed the call of doctors and hospitals, and prepared bandages and lint. But through all business or idleness there ran a current of excitement not by any means unpleasant—the excitement of playing a great part, with all Europe for spectators.

One day Pauline received a note from Vilpont—a few lines, advising her to display the Geneva flag from her window, and to prepare beds for the wounded in her outhouses. The sight of his handwriting, and the conviction which she now had—that he, in a manner,

11

watched over her—moved her beyond concealment. Zelie had remained in the room after
delivering the note, and marked Pauline's
change of color, and the tears that involuntarily filled her eyes. Looking up suddenly
she caught the cat-like, treacherous vigilance
of Zelie's face. The two women stared fixedly
at one another, and Zelie knew that Pauline
had penetrated her secret feelings. Once
fairly put on her self-defence Pauline was no
coward. She said calmly, but with command
in her voice."

"I am advised to hang out a Geneva flag,
and to prepare beds for the wounded."

"And how does madame intend to manage
about the nursing?"

"You will see," was the quiet reply.

That very day, to Zelie's unmistakable annoyance, two sisters of *Bon Secours* came to
stay in the house. One of them was past mid-
dle-age; the other—young, bright, and pretty.
Their companionship gave Pauline a feeling
of protection; and, besides that, they put in
good working-order her crude efforts at organ-
izing a limited hospital. There were not only
beds put in the coach-house, but all the costly
furniture of the great *salon* was removed to
the attics, and a row of small hospital beds lined
each side.

Zelie did not allow this to be done without
protesting, but Pauline, saying, "I alone give
orders here in M. Subar's absence," set her on
one side.

"You now, I by and by," muttered Zelie.

The sisters were like two big children in everything that did not relate to their calling. Chocolate, bon-bons, and oranges had high places in their tariff of pleasures. They delighted in hearing and telling marvellous stories, and though they often alluded to the other world, certainly thoroughly enjoyed this one. If any circumstance brought too vividly to their knowledge that sin, sorrow, suffering existed, they would say something sweet about strayed lambs, or that we should rejoice in tribulation, or that all pain was but for a time. Their spirits were never damped by vivid sympathy; they were too much set apart by their vocation, to enter keenly into the joys or afflictions they came in contact with. Pauline had already noted this same deficiency of human interest in Madame Agnes.

Sister Madeleine. the elder of the two, had an amazing knowledge of bodily ailments. She was a complete pharmacopœia, trotting from morning till night on two sturdy legs. Her only apparent imperfection was a gentle contempt for all other gifts than her own. Pretty Sister Prudence was at this time going through her probation.

Gambetta's departure in a balloon excited both sisters to the highest degree. At the idea of his flying over the head of *ces monstres de Prussiens*, they laughed till they cried, and then wept over the dictator's possible danger, until they were again tickled by the oddity of the situation. Pauline delighted in them, it was so long since she had felt sure of any one about her.

This period of comparative peace and plenty passed away, but not the Germans. The girdle of iron pressed closer and closer, soon followed by decrees limiting supplies of fresh provisions; ambulance-carriages multiplied in number, and were in constant activity. The sisters ceased to have leisure for chattering— no more merry laughs—they went about with the faces that belong to the serious side of nature. All the beds in the outhouses were filled, and many of the *salon*. Every one, from the lady of the house to the scullion, had their hands full. Zelie alone avoided the wounded, and so to her was entrusted the task of providing food for the pretty numerous household.

By the last days of October, the amount of fresh meat allowed to each person was only fifty grammes.

In November, Pauline was applied to for her horses. She gave them at once as a gift.

"What will monsieur say, and he paid so much for them," remonstrated Zelie.

"Monsieur would have done the same, I believe; at any rate, I could not sell the poor animals' lives."

Pauline had sent several balloon letters to her parents, but without receiving any in return. Two long months she had been without any news of them or her husband.

Though Vilpont had never repeated his visit, he had called several times at the lodge of the *concierge* to inquire for her. But now these calls and inquiries ceased. It never came into her mind to fancy the omission proceeded from forgetfulness or negligence. Her woman's instinct would never let her make such a mistake. She guessed at once that he must have taken up a musket, as so many others like him were doing. She reflected long whether any misapprehension of her motives could arise if she sent Joseph to his address to make some inquiries. After hesitating for several days, she suddenly gave Joseph the commission. Zelie, with her usual mocking smile, brought her the answer, that Monsieur le Marquis de Kergeac was on duty with his regiment of Mobiles.

"Then I must let Joseph try to do me the service I intended to ask of M. de Kergeac. Send your husband to me."

"Not so stupid after all," muttered Zelie.

"Joseph," said Pauline, "I have seen a notice that by paying a franc, an answer, yes or no, to four questions, will be conveyed to the provinces from Paris by pigeon. You will go to one of the offices and send the four questions I have written down on this paper."

"Zelie would manage better than I should," said Joseph with a demurring air.

"You can go together if you please," she answered, sick at heart at having no better assistance in her need.

Husband and wife had thought it wiser to obey; no saying what might occur. So in a few days Pauline knew that her father and mother were well, and that they had had news of Léon.

The pigeon carriers played the same part as the agony column of the *Times*. They ought to have earned eternal gratitude from all French people. To kill a pigeon should be classed by them among crimes.

Greater and greater difficulty in obtaining food. The number she fed daily had reduced Pauline's stores alarmingly. The cold was intense, and how could she refuse to share food and fuel with those who had none.

# CHAPTER XII.

## THE CRASH OF LIFE.

THE thirtieth November was a date that, as long as she lives, Pauline will never forget. The date when all the emotions of her being vibrated to their utmost.

Ducrot had succeeded in getting his troops across the Marne, and, after twelve hours' hard fighting, had driven the Prussians from their positions, occupying in the evening the ground held by the enemy in the morning. It might have been expected that Paris would have been greatly agitated by such news, and with the hope that the second day might be equally prosperous. But the truth is, popular feeling rarely follows a logical course. On this St. Andrew's day, when the destiny of the city for good or evil was trembling in the balance, there were no signs of excitement visible in the streets.

Perhaps the intense frost, the biting wind, together with hunger, accounted for the absence of public animation. It is well, surely, that the body should make its weakness felt, so as to numb the anxieties of the heart.

Towards evening, however, multitudes thronged as usual to the different city gates to await the arrival of the ambulance carriages. Pale mothers, wives, children, and graybeards stood with dry, impatient, straining eyes, shuddering with terrified anticipation.

On that evening, for the first time, Pauline went down into the avenue, joining a group that had gathered before her door. All day she had been unusually restless, unable to stay in one place for five minutes together, shrinking with unaccustomed dread from attending on the wounded.

"I feel as if something frightful was about to happen," she said to Sister Madeleine.

"You have done too much, dear madame; you must lie down and rest."

"Lie down!" exclaimed Pauline impatiently, "and be suffocated by this fear that oppresses me."

Sister Madeleine had no time for discussion, but forced Pauline to swallow some *sal volatile*.

With a shawl over her head she stood trembling at her door, catching at every word being bandied about. Now, it was affirmed that Ducrot and all the generals were killed. A second later, there was a hum of triumph. The French were victorious. A man running past, called out, "The Mobiles are massacred —cut down to a man!"

All of a sudden there emerged from out of the darkness a cry of, "*Laissez passer!*" The groups separated right and left, and every one recognized what was a familiar sight— men carrying an hospital stretcher, on which lay a form covered with a sheet.

"Numero 99 ?" asked a voice.

"Here," was answered in chorus, and the court-yard doors were thrown open.

"But we have not a bed vacant," cried Sister Madeleine, running forward with a light in her hand.

"It does not matter; he does not need one. The body was brought in by some of his men, and as this address was fastened on his coat, it has been sent on here."

Already become a thing—an *it*—Sister Madeleine's feeble light fell on the face, from which the hospital aids had lifted the sheet.

Pauline had not needed to see, in order to be sure it was Vilpont.

"Follow me," she said in a quiet voice. "Joseph, run for a doctor."

The bearers looked significantly at the by-standers, but when Pauline reiterated the order, they obeyed. She led them into what had been her boudoir.

"I pray you not to move him till the doctor has come," she said, as they were about to lay the body on the floor.

There was so much pain in her voice, such unimaginable suffering in her look, as none could resist. The men sat down, with a grim compassion.

In another five minutes a doctor came in, but not Dr. M——, who was busy elsewhere. Pauline's eyes were fastened on his face as he leaned over the body, feeling the pulse, applying his ear to the heart. She sickened with

11*

fear when he drew back in silence, but she found strength to say,

" Try to do something," and then she herself began to chafe one of the poor cold hands.

" Take her away," whispered the doctor to the Sister.

Sister Madeleine had store of knowledge of such cases of hope against proof; but to convince Pauline of the usefulness of all effort, she held a small hand-mirror to the lips of the supposed dead man. She started, and signed to the doctor; there was certainly a slight haze on the glass.

" You must leave us, madame," said the doctor.

Pauline held out her hands with a gesture of supplication, and then turned and left the room.

In darkness and solitude Pauline sat for more than an hour. People do not think consecutively in such moments—in fact, their so-called thoughts resemble rather the phantasmagoriæ of dreams. The past, the present, the future mingle in an irrational dance, and, what is stranger still, even while the heart is beat down by anguish the comic element will intrude itself. Look how Hamlet jests with the grave-digger. Assuredly, in this hour, every circumstance that connected her life with Vilpont's, returned to Pauline's recollection, and assuredly more than once a smile passed over her pale lips, as she recalled those pleasant Sundays at Vignes Ste. Marie. But amid all the flickerings of memory, the wavering of hopes and fears, rose one piteous desire to be friends again, to hear him say he forgave her the hardness and coldness with which she had met his kindness in their last interview. Why had she been thus? She shrank from any answer with a flush of shame. How had she dared to be his judge?

At last Sister Madeleine came in. Pauline held up her hand before her face, as we do when dazzled by a sudden light. The tiny, glimmering lamp the Sister carried could scarcely have affected any eyes.

"Well, dear Madame, the poor officer breathes; but oh, *mon Dieu*, how he is wounded! All over I may say—his limbs awfully shattered."

"I am glad," dropped from Pauline's lips, thinking only that he still lived.

"We have not moved him. We got a small bed out of a dressing-room."

"Is he conscious?"

The sister shook her head.

# CHAPTER XIII.

## ONE OF LIFE'S TANGLES.

It was curious but true, during all that month of hard privation, of fatigue, of direful anticipation, of the roar of cannon, the crash of bombs, Pauline was happier than she had ever been. She had set aside self-communing, self-reproaches. Time enough by and by, she said, and gave herself up blindly to a foolish gladness.

As long as Vilpont knew no one, she assisted to nurse him, listening with awe to the gabbling of his delirium—a strange medley, sometimes shocking her, at others making her shed tears.

One evening she had been left to watch him while he slept. It had become an absolute necessity to economize oil and candle—gas was no longer possible; so there was only the faint light from the *veilleuse*, by which she could neither see to read nor work. She had been for some time studying the strange, uncouth shadows made by the pretty furniture of the boudoir on walls and ceiling, when she was roused by a whisper—

"Pauline—madame."

She drew back the bed-curtain.

"I know you," said Vilpont.

"Hush! You must not talk."

The caution was spoken involuntarily, and

her first impulse was to run away. He made an effort to hold out his hand; unresistingly she gave him hers. He turned away his head.

"You are better; you will get well," she said, leaning over him; "but you must not talk or exert yourself until the doctor gives you leave." She drew away her hand.

"Do not leave me;" and as he looked towards her she saw his poor thin cheeks wet with tears.

She was frightened by her own feelings; such a wonderful joy, and yet such a sharp pain, overpowering her.

"I must ring for your real nurse, good Sister Madeleine."

He made no answer.

From this day he began to gather strength; Slowly, indeed, but with few relapses. It was against the excessive weakness caused by loss of blood with which the battle had to be waged. He never did know that Pauline was all but starved to give him more food. She daily grew paler, thinner, happy, poor soul, to give up her strength and beauty for him. But after the evening he had recognized her, she never again watched by his bed; she restricted herself to a daily visit of inquiry, either in company with the doctor and Sister Madeleine; yet she was glad with an unknown gladness. He was there, under the same roof; when night came, she knew she would see him in the morning.

And so the time went on to Christmas. In consequence of the excessive cold, and there being no fuel to spare for heating the churches, no midnight mass was performed. But Pauline, as so many other women did, spent the whole day in church. One feeling gave intensity to another. Never had she prayed more fervently, never felt her spirit so elevated. She mistook her enthusiasm for devotion, but though mistaken, it was in perfect good faith.

In spite of cold and hunger the small shopkeepers had erected the usual New Year booths and stalls along the Boulevards. Very odd presents were made on the 1st of January. Some gave tins of preserved meat, others a little flour; one great man carried to a great lady a paper bag filled with potatoes. These were the gifts of the rich; what the poor gave or received may be easily imagined.

Pauline went out, accompanied by Joseph, that forenoon, to see what she could find for those she sheltered. A curious assortment she brought back, and in triumph, too. A slice of cheese, two eggs, a pound of elephant, some nuts, a patty of unknown contents, and so on.

The *salle à manger* was now her only sitting-room. As she went in loaded with her parcels, a gaunt man, looking like a resuscitated Lazarus, leaning on Sister Madeleine with the one arm he could use, walked a step or two forward to meet her.

" *Voila*," exclaimed Sister Madeleine, in a voice of unmitigated triumph,

" A happy new year!" said the convalescent.

Pauline dropped rather than sat down on the nearest chair, and burst into tears, so closely does joy resemble sorrow.

" *Tiens, tiens, c'est drôle*," observed the sister, and trotted away for her panacea of grief—*Eau de Melisses*.

Very wistful were the looks with which Pauline and Vilpont contemplated each other's faces. Words did not come easily from either, and when he spoke, how poor what he said seemed to him, compared to the feelings swelling his heart.

" You are very pale, very thin," his voice husky with weakness and emotion.

" I am quite, quite well," she answered with a fluttering of her lips that would fain have been a smile. " Even the sound of cannon does not give me such headaches as the exercising did at St. Gloi."

" Ah, St. Gloi!" he sighed; and added, "you would have done better to take my advice and return there, though perhaps it would have been worse for me."

" Not a perhaps in the case at all," she said, with some of her old girlish petulance, and a faint flush restored for a moment her girlish prettiness.

But the time was gone past when her beauty, or lack of it, could make any differ-

ence in Vilpont's sentiments towards her. No
one knows how love comes. Sometimes with
a sudden shock like lightning in a dark night,
sometimes growing slowly as the flower from
the seed. The tender preference which Vilpont, in spite of many follies, had always
cherished for Pauline, was now a love that
filled his life. He had no hopes, no projects;
he was content, as it were, to have the void of
his heart filled, even though it might be with
bitter pain. She was worth it, and better regret what is sweetest and best, than have a
joy which leaves remorse and a longing to
forget.

Pauline's feelings, being those of a woman,
were more complex.

> "A little thing it seemed to *her* to fight
> Against hard things, that *she* might see the light
> A little longer, and rejoice therein."

A strange, unreal life it was for these two
during the following three weeks. You might
say it was as if they were playing parts in
some drama picturing domestic happiness.
Many a time Vilpont would feign to be asleep,
for then Sister Madeleine would slip away,
and leave Pauline on guard. He loved to
watch, from under his half-closed lids, the little figure coiled up in the depths of a large
easy chair. He had felt far more passionate
emotion in past years, but had never been
moved by such deep tenderness as for Pauline.
His heart melted within him at the sight of

the small, thin fingers laboring at coarse
shirts for the soldiers; he had scarcely known
so keen an enjoyment as when her large, soft
eyes suddenly flashed angrily at the sound of
any noise which might disturb him. Tears
welled up from his eyes when she frowned
back an intruder. These were signs he could
not mistake; they did him good, brought out
all the latent generosity of his character. He
was as much on his guard with her, as though
he had feared she was capable of treachery.

They talked freely on every subject, except
of the past. All that the keenest, bitterest observer could have laid to their charge was
that their eyes brightened, their lips smiled
when they met. But these hours of half pain,
half joy, were counted.

By the 23d of January, Paris had reached
starvation point, even for those who had
money. Tumults and disorders of various
kinds were of daily occurrence. National
Guards seized on the rations meant for the
very poor, and it was evident as daylight that
worse was in store, should there be no capitulation, and yet it was equally dangerous to
hint at such a possibility.

The circle of attack pressed closer and
closer, the firing grew daily more murderous.

Hints were ventured on in the *Journal
Officiel* that the situation was becoming un-
tenable. Then a note of unmistakable warning sounded. A copy of Prussian despatches
was published—Chanzy, Faidherbe, Bourbaki,

all defeated. Help for Paris from without, a vain imagination. Patience and heroic effort had reached their limit. Must men perish like rats in a trap? That, or the alternative of capitulation.

Poor Pauline, how all the rumors current tortured her. Was the end indeed come, and was there nothing before her but vain regrets, nothing better to wish for than to forget?

As for Vilpont, the news of the approaching capitulation seemed to have dealt his death-blow. Drops of agony fell from his brow as he sat in his helplessness reading the accounts of the pending negotiations. All *his* feelings at that moment were engrossed by the national calamity.

"Oh, that I had died at my post!" he exclaimed over and over again.

He had no thought, no recollection, but of the humiliation of his country.

Very perfect love there may be between man and woman, never perfect sympathy. Man feels and acts independently, woman through man.

With a spasm of pain Pauline recognized how different were their feelings. Above and beyond all *her* grief for the woes of her country, was anguish for her coming severance from him. *He* had forgotten *that his* cry of grief was for France alone, humiliated France.

True woman, alike in her nobleness as in her weakness, she fought against her pain, soothing him with sweet, patient words.

# CHAPTER XIV.

## NOUGHT'S HAD WHEN ALL IS DONE.

THE sacrifice was accomplished—Paris had capitulated. Nevertheless the sufferings of the population were not yet at an end. For many a day bread continued black and disgusting, and all food difficult to be obtained.

On the other hand, there was a plentiful supply of "orders of the day," complimenting army, National Guards, and Mobiles. It was highly satisfactory to them that the world should be informed that the heroic city had succumbed to famine alone.

Astonishing how quickly the routine of public life was restored! The newspapers were full of official decrees nominating ministers, mayors, secretaries—every available wall was covered with gayly colored placards containing the addresses of candidates to electors.

Postal communication was also re-established between the provinces and the capital, and as soon as possible Pauline received letters from Léon and her mother. She ought to have been glad, but she turned white as paper when they were put into her hand.

Léon wrote affectionately, but evidently with restraint. M. Rendu, he said, would set off in two days to bring her to St. Gloi. For some good reasons it had been decided that it was better for him not to go just now to Paris. Pauline did not see Vilpont till the afternoon.

" Papa is coming to-morrow to take me away." She had determined to speak cheerfully, and she did so; but the next moment she lost her self-command, and, bursting into tears, ran out of the room.

After this she saw little of Vilpont. If she went into the dining-room, where he was, she left it again almost immediately. She excused her restlessness by laying it to the account of preparations for her journey.

But he marked and understood every involuntary sign of heart-sickness—the wide opened eyes, strained to keep back tears; the drooping, quivering lips; the sentences begun so bravely, dying away unfinished.

Vilpont was a cool-headed, experienced man of the world, with, when he so chose it, a perfect mastery over himself. As he sat thinking of Pauline, and of her vain struggle to conceal her feelings from him, the thought would intrude of how such and such a one would ridicule his not taking all the advantages of the situation. But our actions are as often determined by the character of those we have to deal with as by our own. Has not some one written that love, like the cameleon, takes the hue of what it feeds on? At any rate, the feeling Pauline had inspired brought out all that was generous and honorable in Vilpont.

It was late, past the hour when they usually said good-night, and yet Pauline lingered.

Sister Madeleine's evening doze had been comfortably prolonged, through the long silences of her companions.

"Will you come nearer to my sofa?" asked Vilpont; and as Pauline took the chair he pointed to, he went on—"There are many things which I long to say to you, and yet it may be as well to leave them unsaid."

"Never mind telling me," faltered Pauline. She drew her breath hard, and added, "You will remain here, of course. The Sisters have agreed to stop with my poor invalids. I should"—— The small, thin hands were clasped together—a gesture of pain and entreaty.

"I will do whatever you wish," he replied very gently.

"Let me hear of your recovery." She spoke sharply and quickly, in a manner quite unlike herself.

"Surely," he answered. "May I tell you my plans for the future?" He was so touched, nay, his worldly armor so transpierced by her anguish, that what he said came from the inspiration of the moment. She bowed her head, listening, with her hands covering her face.

"I shall go to Brittany as soon as I am able. While I was ill and sleepless, I used often to watch the shadows cast on the walls of your boudoir by the pretty furniture—grotesque, ugly shadows—and it came into my mind that so it is with many alluring joys and pleasures, that they also have ugly attendant shadows. Whatever may remain of my life, I promise shall be free of pleasures that have such grim followers."

She made no answer. A hand of iron seemed to be pressing on her throat. He longed to snatch her to his breast to tell her he loved her with a love he had never felt for any other woman. With a rare self-immolation he put aside the temptation. Some say that temptation is only resisted when not strong enough; but Vilpont was accustomed to yield to weak as well as strong temptation. In this case his heroism was complete.

Presently he spoke again, and with well-assumed cheerfulness. "I have not forgotten your criticism of my play. You have shown me the beautiful side of life, and you have my undying gratitude."

She shook her head. Poor soul! she could see no beauty in life at that moment. He also lapsed into silence. Just then Sister Madeleine snored so loud that she woke herself.

" *Tiens!* I have been asleep, and kept my poor monsieur up so late. Madame, you should have roused me."

"Scold me—I alone am in fault," said Vilpont. There was a strange break in his voice as he strove to speak gayly.

Pauline did not wait even to say good-night.

—" I shall die ! —I shall die ! " she said aloud, as she threw herself on her bed.

" Has madame heard any bad news ? " asked Zelie's steady, cold voice.

" Go—I must be alone ; go, go, go ! "

# CHAPTER XV.

### PATHWAYS HERE DIVIDE.

WHEN the capitulation of Paris became a matter only of shorter or longer time, Madame Rendu, with her usual determination to see her way clearly, entered on the discussion of future plans with her son-in-law. A difficult task, for Léon was one of those who have no objection to the provisional, and a very decided aversion *de mettre les points sur les i*——*s*.

He found it vain, however, to attempt to parry the straight thrusts of his adversary, and, forced to his knees, had to make a clean breast of it. From his confession it was obvious that his fine fortune was wrecked, only enough saved to afford his wife and himself the mere necessaries of life. After many twistings and turnings, in an effort to escape his doom, he at last consented that the hotel in Paris, and its costly furniture, should be sold as soon as a purchaser could be found, and that he and Pauline should make their future home in her father's house.

" I suppose you will not object to our having Zelie and Joseph ? " said Léon ; " Pauline must have a maid."

" Neither of those Algerines cross my threshold," returned Madame. " I was unwilling to

interfere before, as Pauline did not complain
—*that* you owed either to her simplicity or
her goodness; nevertheless, it was unpardona-
ble in you ever to bring that woman to my
daughter's house."

"Why!" asked Léon in a raised voice.

But madame was not inclined to explain.
She restricted her answer, like the clever
woman she was, to a repetition of her verdict.

"Manage how you like, neither Joseph nor
his worse half come here."

They were standing at a window which
looked into the front court (for the Rendu's
house was one between *cour et jardin*), and
they saw Madame de Saye coming in.

"Ask Madame de Saye for her opinion of
your *protégée*," added Madame Rendu.

"You have just come *à propos*, my dear
Stephanie," said madame. "We are discussing whether or not to bring Madame Zelie and
her husband here."

Stephanie held up both her hands, with an
expressive "O madame!"

Madame Rendu smiled.

"That woman made my skin creep," went
on Stephanie; "and I am sure she hates Pauline."

"Now then, Léon, you cannot doubt that
Madame de Saye is an impartial umpire."

"They cannot be sent away at a moment's
notice, as if they were thieves, nor left without money," said Léon sulkily.

"Those are mere details," returned Madame

12

Rendu loftily; "the gist of the affair is their discharge from your service."

" I cannot help myself, as this house is not mine," and he left the room.

" What does he mean ? " asked Stephanie.

" That he has mismanaged his fortune, and must stay here and nurse the remains for years to come. No use trying to make a mystery of what must come to be known. Thank God, Pauline need not feel any loss of comfort."

Though speaking so candidly in this instance, Madame Rendu was capable of keeping secret what need not be known. She could, indeed, as the result proved, really keep a secret—never tell it to human ear.

It happened that by the same post which brought the first letter from Pauline, after the capitulation, had come one for Léon. Madame Rendu had herself taken both from the postman's hands. The address on the letter for Léon was not in his wife's writing; the postmark, however, showed that it had been put into the same box as that from Pauline. Madame Rendu jumped to the immediate conclusion that Zelie had written to M. Subar, and without so much as a moment's hesitation, she opened the envelope, read the contents, then walked to her own room, put it into the fire, and watched until it was entirely consumed.

" Thank God!" she exclaimed, satisfied with her own performance.

" *Que de malheurs eut prévenus le men-*

*songe !*" exclaims a French writer. Madame Rendu agreed in the sentiment and acted upon it.

It was the contents of a very vile letter from Zelie which made Madame Rendu resolve that not Léon but M. Rendu should go to fetch Pauline without delay from Paris. She could not go herself; first, because she thought it absolutely necessary to keep Léon under her own eye; and in the next place, she doubted her self-command holding out in any encounter with Zelie. Much to her surprise, and also to her infinite satisfaction, Léon offered no opposition to her proposal that it should be M. Rendu who went to fetch Pauline. She had made up her mind to employ any means short of murder to prevent a meeting between him and Zelie. He, on his side, was equally desirous to avoid the scenes and reproaches his foster-sister would inflict on him; and dreaded also the concessions she might wring from him.

It was strange, but true, that this unprincipled woman—a mere serving-woman, liable to be discharged as any other domestic—was the pivot on which the future comfort of this family turned; and stranger still, that, save Madame Rendu, no one suspected her power of doing mischief.

One of Léon's messages to his wife concerned her diamonds—she was to bring them with her. These jewels figured prominently in his calculations of the property he could still call his own.

Time never lags when it is bringing the hour of a cruel separation. M. Rendu arrived exactly when he was expected, and the day following Pauline was to return to St. Gloi. Her father was shocked at her appearance: she was thin to emaciation, with that look of premature age which severe suffering often gives to a youthful face. But what alarmed him most was the alternate excitement and prostration of her spirits. She would ask him question on question, and forget to listen to his answers. He watched her with hourly increasing dread and remorse. He could not hide from himself that he had failed to defend, while it was yet time, his child's happiness—that he had yielded it up from weakness, not ignorance. The pang that now wrung his heart was the recoil of the blow he had helped to inflict. He learned the lesson we all have to learn, that the ill we do is never unfruitful—we must share its consequences. He learned that any failure to respect the rights and feelings of our fellows is sure to weigh forever on the conscience.

M. Rendu agreed to all the arrangements Pauline proposed with regard to the Sisters, to the sick, and the servants, reiterating her invitation to Vilpont to remain where he was as long as convenient to him. He neither thwarted her by advice, nor troubled her by opposition. His one paramount wish was to have her once more safely under his roof, away from the peculiar trials of her present position.

"How does madame intend to carry the diamonds?" asked Zelie, ostentatiously displaying them as she spoke.

"My father will take charge of them; they can all go in my hand-bag."

"And pray, madame, how long are all these people and the nurses to remain here?"

"Till the sick are well enough to go away; there are but few remaining now."

"And who is to provide their food, and wait on them?"

"My father will give you any money you require, and the service will go on as if I were here."

"I was engaged to superintend Monsieur Subar's household, and not to attend to people picked up in the streets."

Pauline looked full into the insolent face confronting hers, and said with spirit—

"Zelie, I have borne a good deal from you on Monsieur Subar's account, but now I tell you plainly that you will never again be in my service."

"Madame has no power to discharge me. I take no dismissal but from Monsieur Subar; and if madame would take my advice, it would be not to make me her enemy."

"Do you think friends are manufactured through fear, Zelie?" and Pauline looked at her with a smile of pity. "However, the

question is not one that interests me just now.
Be so good, when you have put the diamonds
into the bag, to bring me the key, and lock the
dressing-room door inside. After that I shall
not require to see you again."

Zelie answered with a sulky "Bien, madame."
Every tinge of color had left her cheeks.

Pauline hurried away, more frightened than
she would have liked to confess.

It was evening before M. Rendu sent for
Joseph; he thought it best to deal with the
man alone. In fact, Joseph had always
behaved respectfully to Madame Subar. His
fault was the allowing his wife to guide
him against his better feeling—a fault for
which M. Rendu might have a sympathetic
compassion.

Joseph was dumbfoundered at receiving his
dismissal and Zelie's in settled terms.

Madame Rendu had persuaded Léon to
copy with his own hand the letter she had
prepared for him. She had made no objection
to the sum he proposed to pay yearly to Zelie;
nor to his paying their way back to Algiers
if they chose to return thither. She had
made up her mind that to get rid of these
people some sacrifice of money would be inevitable.

"When must we leave, sir?" asked Joseph.

"There is no immediate hurry—at your
convenience. You and your wife will go
over the inventory with the person Monsieur
Subar employs to effect a sale of this house

and furniture. Monsieur and Madame Subar will reside with us at St. Gloi, and thus, you understand, will not require your services. Everything will be done by Monsieur Subar to render this change no loss to you."

With a polite "Good-night," and not a little pleased at having accomplished this disagreeable business so easily, M. Rendu went up to the room he was to occupy—close to that of his daughter.

# CHAPTER XVI.

### DARK HOURS.

THE strain on Pauline's feelings during that
sad day had worn out what little strength
still remained to her; she was as wearied in
body as though she had walked ten miles.
Nevertheless, when she went to bed, she did
not at once fall asleep. She was troubled by
all sorts of vague fears. She fancied she
heard stealthy footsteps, the creaking of doors
cautiously opened; then came the distinct
howl of a dog, as it seemed, beneath her
windows. The dim light of her *veilleuse* all
at once gave a sinister splutter, and went out;
and at the same instant it occurred to her that
she had forgotten to lock her bedroom door.
While she lay struggling for courage to get
up and light a candle, heavy sleep overtook
her. She knew afterwards that she could not
have slept more than a few minutes when she
was awoke by a loud crash. At the first
moment Pauline took the sound for the familiar one of the bursting of a bomb, a palpable
danger she could face. She seized her bell, and
continued ringing it till she heard the hurrying
of many feet on the stairs. Then she jumped
up, lighted her candle, and hurrying on a dressing gown, joined the group gathered on the
landing before her door.

M. Rendu was a droll enough sight in his nightcap, and Sister Madeleine was not behind him in the grotesqueness of her gear. Joseph, too, with his head in a yellow *foulard* was more like a gorilla than a smart valet; but every one was too much alarmed to be tickled by one another's appearance.

"Look there!" suddenly cried Sister Madeleine, raising her arm with a gesture *à la Siddons.*

Instead of looking, every one huddled together, and strove not to see what might be some direful sight.

The splendid mirror on the first landing of the great staircase was shivered from top to bottom. At the foot of the stairs lay a bedroom candlestick, the candle it had held some yards off. It was perfectly clear that the candlestick had been hurled right into the centre of the mirror.

But by whom?—and why?

Sister Madeleine came quietly to M. Rendu, and showed him something she had picked up. It was one of those curved Algerine daggers used by the common people in Algeria.

"Joseph," called out M. Rendu, holding up the dagger in the sight of all, "does this belong to you?"

Joseph looked and trembled: "I know nothing about how it came here, sir."

"I miss your wife," put in Sister Madeleine.

"Is Zelie not with you, Madame?" asked the poor fellow, turning to Pauline.

12*

" I have not seen her since the afternoon," said Pauline.

" Go and look for her, Joseph," said M. Rendu. " And now, my good friends," he continued, " let us all go back to our beds, and thank God there is no greater harm done than the breaking of a mirror."

As Pauline and her father were going up-stairs, Sister Madeleine came close to them, and whispered, " That woman did it, and from sheer terror. I know of a man, who, after he had murdered his master and mistress, mistook his own face in a glass he was passing for some one else, and threw the bloody knife at his own reflection—he confessed it after-wards."

" Pray do not tell me anything more," said Pauline, " but stay with me till morning. I am too frightened to be alone."

" I will send you Sister Prudence. I must go back and quiet Monsieur le Marquis. I turned the key on him when I ran out on hearing the bell ring so violently. Lucky all the invalids are out of the *salon;* a fine busi-ness it might have been with all those men looking on!" and away bustled Sister Made-leine.

It was a most mysterious occurrence. The bag containing the diamonds lay on the toilette-table as Pauline had seen it when she went to bed. The small key was in her purse; the lock was a patent one, and it was quite intact.

Could Zelie have contemplated a crime worse than robbery?—and if so, what had de-deterred her?

"Do not send for the police, papa," said Pauline; "what does a cracked glass matter. If you do, we shall be detained. Let us get away from that terrible woman, or something worse will happen."

Sister Madeleine was convinced some mischief had been done, though not yet discovered. "Was Madame Subar sure she had her diamonds?"

"There's the key, and there's the bag," said Pauline.

"Will you not look to see they are really in the bag?" persisted the sister.

Pauline hesitated, changing color rapidly. Then she said slowly, "No; if they are stolen, as I see you suspect, papa will send for the police, and she will come back and do what she meant to do last night—I cannot venture. O Sister Madeleine! help me to get away."

There was nothing to be said in answer to such an appeal, and Sister Madeleine tried to be satisfied by repeating that it was no business of hers. Vilpont also was unwilling to let the matter rest without further investigation; but he also felt he had no right to press his advice on M. Rendu and his daughter.

The last moment—that terrible last moment of farewell—came with its hard punctuality. Pauline went into the *salle à manger* leaning on her father's arm to say good-by to Vilpont.

She had left herself but a few short minutes. "I shall get through it, because I must," she had kept on all the morning saying to herself, with a dread as to her own strength.

Vilpont saw the shudder that was shaking the whole thin form. With a sad effort at self-command, he said, "Bon voyage, chère madame."

She said nothing, just glanced towards him.

They parted as well-bred acquaintance might have done.

# CHAPTER XVII.

## TWO WAYS OF LOOKING AT THINGS.

"IT's nobody's business but ours."

Few among us have not said this once at least in our lives, and probably with always the same result of finding that our neighbors insist on having a finger in our pie.

Madame Rendu ought to have known better than to make such a speech. Nevertheless, she did say those very words to her husband.

Poor lady! she had to submit to be questioned, and to explain why *this* had happened and why *that* had not, as if her interrogators had been so many *juges d'instruction.* She was, however, equal to the occasion, and admirable alike in her reticences as in her confidences.

Undoubtedly glad as they were to have Pauline safely back among them, the St. Gloisians felt they had some right to resent her inopportune seclusion.

"It is according to the doctor's orders, I assure you," said Madame Rendu. "He has sent her to bed, and desired she should be kept as quiet as possible."

"One would have thought the happiness of being again with her husband would have been her best doctor," observed Madame Chambaud.

" Poor Monsieur Subar says Pauline is only nervous, and that Madame Rendu encourages her in thinking herself ill." That was Stephanie's account—and every one joined in the chorus of " Poor Monsieur Subar !"

Léon being thus an object of commiseration, became more popular than ever.

In the privacy of her own room, alone with M. Rendu, madame indemnified herself for all the restraint she endured in public.

" Such fair prospects, and all lost—Léon throwing away a princely fortune like an idiot ; Pauline fretting herself to death ; and *that* man (alluding to Vilpont) spared when so many worthier were killed. It's like a doom on us."

Madame Rendu's disappointments were undeniable. But she had this comfort, that she attributed them entirely to the faults of others, and honestly believed herself clear of all mistakes or blame.

" I begin to doubt the wisdom of parents choosing for their children," said M. Rendu.

The assertion of such a doubt by her husband struck Madame Rendu dumb for some seconds. Then she said with the firmness that conviction gives, " It's not our system that is wrong, but the half-measures that have gained ground among us. Girls should be married as they were formerly, before mixing in the world."

" It's a puzzle," sighed M. Rendu.

" No puzzle to me," she said. " Parents

must be the best judge of what is best for their children, or what is the use of having experience."

"Indeed, my dear, I have come to have little faith in the uses of experience, whether in the government of a family or of a nation."

"Ah! well, thank God I have no more daughters to marry."

When Madame Rendu heard of what had occurred on the night of Zelie's disappearance, she said, "I am afraid, Léon, your *protégée* has had no faith in your promises, and has helped herself to a provision for her future wants. Depend on it the diamonds will not be found in the bag."

"We shall see that. I would stake my life on Zelie's honesty," he replied hotly.

"Take care, my son, take care," retorted the lady; "such warmth is suspicious. Where is the bag?"

It was in Pauline's room, and there it was opened. At the sight of the jewel-cases, Léon exclaimed triumphantly, "You see, madame! Ah! poor Zelie."

Madame Rendu was surprised, and it must be owned to her credit that she was not vexed at being proved wrong.

Léon drew forth the cases with the loving hand of proprietorship. He opened one, and set it down as if it had burned his fingers. He took out another and another—alas! all empty.

It was the first time in her life that Madame Rendu had been moved to unseemly mirth;

but at the sight of Léon's appalled face she burst into loud laughter.

He looked at her in alarm.

"Don't be frightened, I am not in hysterics. Poor Léon! how lucky your life does not depend on that yellow woman's honesty."

It gratified her feminine instincts to note Zelie's personal defects.

"How do you know Zelie was the thief?" asked Léon in a fierce voice. He was smarting under two blows—betrayed confidence, and a great loss of property. His words were an outcome of pain, and had no definite meaning. He stopped literally from terror, at the fury in Madame Rendu's eyes. She also was writhing under the dominion of a hidden wound.

"You are very hard on me," said Léon after a pause. "You should make allowances for a man in such trouble. Even Pauline does not seem to care what happens to me, and yet it is her fault."

Pauline had hitherto kept silence; her poor pale face, white as the pillow it lay on, ought to have pleaded against any attack. Now she said, "I do care very much; and, Léon, you do not know how painful it was to me to have Zelie put as it were in power over me. I bore it patiently, to please you."

"I am never likely to have power to do anything I please again," he said, and left the room.

"A hundred thousand francs gone at one stroke!" exclaimed Madame Rendu, as she gathered together the pretty, velvet-lined cases.

The theft of the diamonds was not to be concealed; it was the town talk, and everybody's business. Stephanie de Saye had the satisfaction of saying, morning, noon, and night, "I told Pauline how it would be. I warned her against that woman, but she would not listen to me; and now I should not wonder if all her illness comes from some African poison."

That was easy of belief; but what no one could understand was the hesitation shown by the Subars and Rendus in putting the matter into the hands of the police. M. Rendu, indeed, was at first urgent to do so, but Pauline pleaded hard against any step of the kind being taken.

"She meant to kill me that night, papa. If you let her alone, she will keep out of our way; If you attack her, I shall never be safe."

To M. Rendu's amazement, and to that of Léon, Madame Rendu supported Pauline's views.

"It's paying dear for immunity," she said, " but we shall be free of her pitch." That destroyed letter to Léon rankled in her mind. For worlds she would not have Pauline and Zelie brought as adversaries before a public tribunal. An unprincipled, dishonest woman would stick at no calumny to revenge herself.

As for Léon, he could be got to say nothing further than, " Do as you please; as I said before, I have now no power."

How it would have ended no one can tell. The story might have spread far, and justice might have interfered whether the injured parties wished it or not ; but the ill wind which raised the Commune put an effectual stop to all proceedings in this matter.

    .        .        .        .        .

Two years have gone by, and the Subars still make their home with M. and Mme. Rendu. Léon's ambition is satisfied with being the mirror of fashion in St. Gloi—the admired of all beholders. So true is it that we are constantly changing the scale by which we measure the happiness or unhappiness of our life.

Nothing more has been heard of Zelie or the diamonds.

Madame de Saye's last piece of news is that the Marquis de Kergeac is at Rome, and is about to take the vows in the Dominican convent there.

These two years have worn smooth the rough side of Pauline's sorrow. A great grief brings in its train repose. All pain, all longing, must have an end ; we die or we grow resigned.

At first Pauline sought for comfort in the practice of severe penances. She tried to harden herself by a constant combat against self-pity. She did daily battle with her inclinations. When she would have welcomed solitude, she went into society ; when silence would have been grateful to her, she conversed. Hearts can be very sad, very repentant, while the lips smile and the tongue talks pleasantly ;

just as there may be a hair shirt beneath gauze and lace.   She had set herself to win a victory, undertaken the greatest of all conquests, that of her rebellious heart ; undertaken to bring her feelings into subjection to duty. Who can doubt her ultimate triumph, when her war-cry is—*God will, I shall.*

"Prayers are the daughters of Jupiter," said the ancients.   The moderns say, " *Hoc vult Deus.*"